DEMONIC DESIRES

DESTINY DIESS

Copyright © 2020 Destiny Diess.

All rights reserved. This book or parts thereof may not be reproduced in any form, stored in any retrieval system, or transmitted in any form by any means— electronic, mechanical, photocopy, recording, or otherwise—without prior written permission of the author, except as provided by United States of America copyright law. For permission requests, write to the author, at "Attention: Permissions Coordinator," at the email address below.

Any references to historical events, real people, or real places are used factiously. Names, characters, and places are products of the author's imagination.

Front cover image by Lena B. Wolf.

Typography supplied by WeGotYouCoveredBookDesign

Beta Team: Abby Gibson, Kayla Lutz, Madi Lozada, Diana Klíková, Lauren Greenwell, MaKenzie Blank, Erin Krakow

First printing edition 2020.

Destiny Diess

destinydiess@gmail.com

www.destinydiess.com

❀ Created with Vellum

TO ALL THE QUEENS AND KINGS OF
LUST.

CHAPTER 1

My castle. My kingdom. My Eros.
He pushed me against our balcony doors, kissing me from behind. Lips against my neck. Fingers trailing up and down my sides. Hardness pressed against my back. I curled my fingers into the curtains and grasped them in my hand, enjoying this blissful moment with the only man I wanted.

"Out," he said, clutching the door handle. "I want everyone to watch me devour every inch of your body."

I pushed the doors open, expecting to see the beautiful Kingdom of Lust that I had woken up to for almost two weeks now. But instead of the rosy exterior, everything was burning with red flames that licked the edges of the balcony, orange lava that surrounded the castle, and black ash that rained down from the fiery sky above us and burned when it touched my skin. He placed his hands on the balcony next to me, trapping me between him, and drew his nose up the side of my neck.

"Dani," he said, his voice so utterly sensual. God, I wanted him. If I could, I'd take all of him... every last piece, savor every single taste, let him become a part of me. He curled a hand around the front of my throat, squeezing gently. "You don't know how fucking long I've waited for you to find me." He squeezed tighter, pushed me against the railing

1

—my breasts pressing against the edge—and drew his fingers harshly against my nipples, sending a wave of pleasure through me.

God, Eros always knew the exact way I needed to be touched.

When he flicked his long fingernails against one of them again, I moaned softly to myself and grasped the black balcony. Flames licked my fingers, but I didn't care. His heat was already too much for me.

He pressed himself against my backside, letting me feel his cock against my ass. Distant, hazy memories that I barely even remembered flashed through my mind, like his hands wrapped around my throat, using my body to thrust into me. Him putting a collar around my neck and walking me down the Lust Room hallway in our castle to his room. Tying my wrists to the headboard and my ankles to the footboard of a familiar bed and slapping me hard against the cheek when I refused to suck his cock.

Those long, calloused fingers brushed down my arm, making my hair stand up. Though it must've been over a hundred degrees here, his touch made me shiver. So familiar yet so utterly foreign.

He interlocked his fingers with mine on the balcony, pressing them against my family ring and squeezing them tightly. After shuddering for the briefest moment, he slipped his hand into my panties and rubbed my clit, finally giving me what I wanted.

"I'll take everything from you, Dani." He breathed harshly against my ear, two fingers thrusting hard up inside of my wet pussy. I clenched around him, loving the way he used me. "Ruin your perfect little body." A wave of pleasure rolled through me. "Destroy all those heavenly thoughts running through your mind." Pressure built higher in my core. "Corrupt you."

I doubled over the balcony, grasping the railing to hold myself up despite my trembling legs. He brushed his fangs against my neck and chuckled. "You've cum already? I haven't even started yet."

There was more to his words, yet I didn't bother trying to figure it out now. All I could see were flames, me standing in the flames with a crown on my head, fire in my eyes, and a kingdom that burned brightly behind me...

He tugged on my ring, nearly taking it off of me, and continued to touch my pussy, his fingers moving faster than before. "In two weeks you'll ascend as Queen and Commander of Lust, and once you do... this kingdom will become yours and Lust will become mine." Something in his voice seemed so irate and tense.

He smirked against my neck, his fangs pricking the skin, nearly drawing blood. I gazed down from our balcony, watching the black and white ash fall from the eerie red clouds above. It fell onto my skin, no longer burning it but becoming part of me, clinging onto it like it was supposed to be there.

But... this kingdom wasn't Lust.

My head felt fuzzy, and I swayed in Eros's arms. He pulled his fingers out of me and rubbed them against my clit again. I grasped the railing tighter. "Oh, my god."

"God won't help you down here, my Ira."

"Please," I whispered.

"Please, what?"

A wave of heat washed over me, making my cheeks flush. "Eros," I breathed, my mind in a daze. All I could feel was the intense pressure in my core and his hard cock against me. I wanted him inside of me. God, I wanted him inside of me so bad. "Eros, please."

"Eros?" he asked with so much distaste on his tongue. I tensed for the briefest moment, my mind beyond cloudy. "Still so innocent, Dani... you don't know the first thing about stealing souls, the first thing about taking a life, the first thing about leading a kingdom."

My brows furrowed. What... what was he talking about?

"Eros is long gone. It's just me and you in this pretty little mind of yours."

"Wh-what do you mean Eros is..." My heart beat against my chest. I turned around in his embrace and shrieked. Two alluring maroon eyes stared down at me, the same eyes that had been haunting my memory for the past two weeks.

Javier.

DESTINY DIESS

Javier was here. Javier was back. How was he back? Why was here, in my dream?

He smirked and stepped toward me, pinning me to the balcony, wrapping his hand around my throat, and letting the flames burn my flesh. "You're mine now, Dani." He inched closer and closer and closer, yet I couldn't move back. It seemed as if I was stuck in a nightmare. His lips brushed against mine. "All mine."

CHAPTER 2

I sat up in my empty bed and screamed at the top of my lungs. Oh, god. Oh, god. Oh, god. What the hell was that? Where was Eros? Why was I dreaming of Javier?

My heart thumped loudly against my chest, and I hopped out of bed, suddenly feeling beyond hot. The window was cracked slightly, the pink sunlight pouring in through it. I stumbled over to the balcony and pushed the doors open just enough to see my kingdom. The beautiful pink hills, the plush sky, the velvet rose garden. Not that atrocity from my dream.

But that... that wasn't just any normal dream. That was a lust dream, a dream intricately woven and forged by an incubus himself. An incubus who was supposed to be dead.

Dreaming of Javier—*like that*—was impossible.

After drawing my thumb against my family ring, I took a deep breath. Maybe it was all just a nightmare. Yeah, that's what it was. It had to be. Javier couldn't be back. I was just getting too deep in my own head. All the stress from transitioning to Hell, from ascending as queen in a couple of weeks, from Kasey refusing to talk to me because Eros killed their parents.

DESTINY DIESS

Someone knocked on the bedroom door. "Commander, is everything okay? Should I get Eros?" Esha, the guard Eros had assigned to our chambers, asked.

I tied my scarlet silk robe around my waist and tried to think about better days. When Mom would wake me up with a big plate of French toast and a huge grin on Sunday mornings, when we'd visit the ice skating rink and twirl around on the ice for hours, when she smiled at me.

"Commander Asmodeus?"

"I'm fine," I said, gazing out the balcony doors. Demons walked down the white stone walkways from the palace to the nearest town, Chastion, below me. It was only eight in the morning, and some of them were stumbling home from a late night down in the palace's Lust Rooms. The parties raged on until early in the mornings; the demons had been drinking Passion Delights on the front stairs and had been staggering through the castle.

I grasped the curtains. My quiet life had been replaced by boozing and partying in just a few short days. The Kingdom of Lust was nothing like the city back home...

But maybe I needed the change. I couldn't stay with Maria for the rest of my life. Dad liked it here, so I would try to like it too.

"Eros wanted me to inform you that he will be in the Garden of Passion, waiting for you."

After changing into something more modest—not that anyone would care—I opened the bedroom door. Dressed in a tight leather uniform that only the highest-ranked Lust guards wore, Esha nodded at me. "Good morning, Asmodeus."

I brushed my fingers against her wrist. "Please, just Dani," I said. She followed me down the hundreds of spiraling stairs to the ground floor. "Have you heard from Kasey?"

"No."

"Aarav?"

"No."

6

DEMONIC DESIRES

I pressed my lips together. "Mycah?"

"Unfortunately, no."

After sighing through my nose, I nodded my head and walked out of the castle doors. She followed me, because Eros asked her to follow me everywhere, but I stopped her—my mind still buzzing with those dreadful thoughts from this morning. "I will find Eros alone."

I just needed time to breathe.

Once she walked back inside the castle, I hurried along the stone pathway toward the Garden of Passion. The Garden of Passion was a luscious rose garden near Chastion. I pushed around people to get there as quickly as possible, to see Eros— my Eros—and to get Javier out of my mind.

Even when Javier was dead, he still found a way to fuck with me.

A group of Lusts blocked the walkway in front of me, and I patiently waited for them to move while I not-so-patiently tried to calm my racing heart. I didn't understand why I had dreamt of Javier, and I didn't think I ever would. Eros had done more than enough to please me. I didn't need to dream of the one man both Eros and I hated the most.

"The crowning ceremony is only in two weeks," one Lust in front of me said.

"I heard from Biast that once she ascends, Sathanus promised to rain fireballs down on her for killing his heir."

My eyes widened, and I slowed my pace. Sathanus, the Commander of Wrath, was promising to kill me, to slaughter me, and to steal *my* soul. Rumors like this had been buzzing around Chastion for a couple weeks now, but I had only heard it from Eros and Esha when they talked to each other. Hearing it from an actual resident of Lust... made me feel things I shouldn't.

Shame. Pain. Outrage.

"Do you think she can rule? Nobody has ever even seen her

alone without Eros in the town yet." They began whispering to each other, and I fell further back, not wanting them to know that I had heard every word of their conversation, because, well, I didn't know what to say. It was true. I hadn't been out to town alone. I hadn't been anywhere in Hell alone. Though the people themselves didn't freak me out, I just didn't fit into their image of me.

I cut through the grass and made a bee-line for the garden. Don't let this get into your head, Dani. Don't let this pile up too. You will be a great queen. You will rule this kingdom with all the might that Dad knew you would. You will not fuck this up.

After clutching my ring so tightly in my palm, I entered the garden. It was empty, yet the sweet scent of cinnamon drifted in through my nostrils. I followed it through the garden, needing Eros to calm me down. The thought of Sathanus only brought me back to Javier, and it seemed that he was all I could think about these last couple of days.

Maybe it was because he was the first person who I had ever killed or maybe it was the fact that I knew he wouldn't be my last. Controlling my demon was far harder than I ever expected. I had thought about sucking Eros's soul too many times to count lately, and I could feel that everyday I was on the verge of breaking.

"Dani," Eros whispered. I turned my head toward the direction of his voice, but he wasn't there. So, I continued walking through the garden of roses, my fingers brushing against each one, letting their scent drift into my nose.

"Dani, come here," he whispered again. I turned around, strands of my dark hair blowing into my face. The pink sun shimmered down onto the rose petals, making them glimmer. I heard him chuckle from behind me and went to turn around, but two strong arms curled around my waist from behind before I could. "If you want to find me, you'll have to be faster than that," Eros said into my ear. He pressed his lips against my collarbone.

DEMONIC DESIRES

"Or, next time, I'll have the chance to corrupt this pretty little mind of yours before you can stop me."

I laughed, tilting my head to brush my lips against his. "And how will you corrupt me, exactly?" I turned in his embrace, drawing a finger up his abdomen. "Make me beg for you? Take me out on one of those bus rides again? Invite Lucifer over?"

His lip curled into a smirk, his eyes dancing with excitement. "I was thinking... force-feed you Fervor Crisps"—He held up a picnic basket full of baked goods and a bottle of Passion Delight—"and let you devour a whole bottle of Passion Delight, but..." He stepped closer to me and brushed his nose against mine. "... your way sounds much more exciting."

After inhaling his cinnamon and forgetting all about Javier's licorice stench from my dream, I relaxed and tugged Eros into a hug, letting my head rest against his chest. I had the strong urge to burst out in tears. It had only been a few days here, and the pressure of everything was almost too much to handle. But I sucked it up because I was *going* to become queen.

Eros's chest rumbled softly, and he curled his arms around me. "I have a spot for us picked out under the cherry tree. We can eat breakfast, enjoy Passion Delights, and help you *relax.*"

I arched a brow and stared up at him, grinning. "It's eight in the morning. We can't have Passion Delights now."

"We can if you say we can, my little Succubus." He grabbed my hand and led me through the garden of roses to a picnic blanket under the blossoming cherry tree. Pink little leaves had fallen onto the blanket. I sat down and pulled out a Fervor Crisp, stuffing it into my mouth and relaxing completely.

Eros gazed at me with his piercing greens. "I heard you had a nightmare."

I chewed my food and looked away from him, scared that he'd see the guilt in my eyes. I wanted to tell him about the dream more than anything... but I couldn't tell him that I had a sex

9

DESTINY DIESS

dream about his brother—the man that I killed. What would he think of me? Worst of all... what would he think of himself?

His parents had beat it into his head that he wasn't a true incubus. If I told him about dreaming of Javier, he'd think all those lies were true. I didn't want to hurt him anymore. I wanted him to heal from their abuse.

"I've been stressing you out lately, haven't I?" he asked, taking a bite into his Fervor Crisp. He eyed the bottle of Passion, but didn't open it. Instead, he just stole another crisp and frowned at me.

I swallowed hard. All I could think about was the Crowning Ceremony and Eros's dire need to be enough for me and my growing urge to suck out his soul and Kasey and Sathanus and... God, it was so much.

"I'm fine, Eros." I clasped my hands together and played with my ring. At least, I needed for everyone to think I was fine, so they trusted me to rule this kingdom. And besides, Javier was just a dream. A stupid, annoying dream. Nothing to worry about right now.

"Don't do that to me," he said, inching closer. "Don't shut me out. Remember, we have to be open with each other if we want this kingdom to thrive. No secrets."

No secrets... but what if I kept one to keep him safe? What if I kept one to keep him from hurting? To keep him from thinking he wasn't enough for me because his parents had told him so much that he wasn't enough that he actually started to believe it?

I sighed through my nose. "It's just the stress of the ceremony. There's so many rumors going around. And, honestly, I don't know if I'll ever be enough for this kingdom. I don't know how I could ever live up to my father's reputation." I gazed around to make sure nobody was listening, then lowered my voice. "Will Lust trust me after all the lies that your family has spewed about my father? And what about when they find out that my mother was an angel?"

DEMONIC DESIRES

Eros placed his Fervor Crisp on the blanket, scooted closer to me, and took my hands in his. "Dani, I don't know what they'll think of you... but I have always believed that you'd be the best to rule this kingdom. I will protect you from anyone who threatens you or your rule."

"I'm nervous," I said.

"Then we'll start your preparations today."

"Preparations?" I asked, brows furrowing. "What kind of preparations? Do I have to memorize every sex position like I had to memorize the periodic table?" Because... Jesus... would that be a disaster.

He chuckled and brushed a strand of hair from my face. "No, preparations for the Courting Pit and for your Courting Ceremony."

My eyes widened slightly. "Courting Pit?"

After pausing for the slightest moment, a look of uneasiness crossed Eros's face. "I didn't want to tell you yet, because it's just going to be added stress, but"—He took a deep breath—"The Courting Pit is where demons can challenge you for your spot as commander."

I nearly choked on my crisp. "Challenge me?" I whispered.

"Yes, and you'll have to prove yourself worthy of the title: Commander of Lust."

"Oh, no, I cannot do that..." I shook my head and put the sweet down on the picnic blanket. Was he crazy?! Did he forget how difficult it was for me to flirt with him when we started dating? "What am I going to have to do? Have sex with people? Flirt with the entire kingdom? Suck them of—"

"We'll start your preparations by flirting." Eros grasped my chin and made me look into his eyes. "Start off slow. Just flirting."

"With who?"

He smirked and then looked at his phone. "We're meeting Lucifer today. In thirty minutes. At the lounge."

Oh, Lord. I had to flirt with Luci? That was bound to go great.

11

DESTINY DIESS

"Don't worry. You're not flirting with him, Dani. Don't rile yourself up yet." He chuckled. "Lucifer just wants to talk."

I raised my brow. Just talk? The Devil never wanted to just *talk*.

CHAPTER 3

*E*ven in the early hours of the afternoon, The Lounge was bustling with women dressed in tiny leather dresses and men in suits. As soon as I stepped into the room, their sweet scents hit my nostrils. I inhaled deeply, eyes closing in delight.

Eros rested his hand on my lower back and guided me through the room to the beige booth that Lucifer reserved. He leaned back in his seat, his icy eyes lively and vibrant as we walked toward him, and raised his glass. "Finally decided to show up."

"Was Lucifer upset we didn't make it here sooner?" I teased, scooting into the seat.

"And if I was?"

I placed a hand on Eros's knee and shrugged my shoulders, giving him a sly smile. "Oh, well."

His wide, excited eyes flickered over to Eros who was arching a brow at me. "Where'd she get this attitude from?"

I kicked my legs back and forth under the table, drawing my fingers against Eros's black jeans. "Eros told me I had to flirt today."

DESTINY DIESS

Lucifer tilted his head toward Eros. "You told your woman to flirt with me?"

"Actually, I told her *not* to flirt with you."

The pretty brunette waitress—who always flirted with me here—leaned over our table to place two Passion Delights in front of us. "Can I get anything else for you, Commander Lucifer, Eros..." She turned to me, her soft, full lips parted ever so slightly.

"Dani," I said to her, my heart rate quickening. She smelt like dark hot chocolate on a chilly day, sweet and needed. "My name is Dani."

"Well, *Dani...*" She brushed her fingers against my forearm, the touch soft and gentle, unlike anything I had felt before. "Can I get you anything else?"

I reluctantly pulled my arm away and shook my head. God, was I bad at this whole flirting thing. I couldn't even look her right in the eye while she was flirting with *me*. It made me feel so... utterly... good. Too good.

Lucifer watched her walk away while *I* focused on the lovely wooden table to try to catch my breath. Eros inhaled deeply, his arm around me relaxing. "Dani," he hummed. "I can sense you."

I pressed my lips together, my cheek flushing a deep red. Lucifer sipped his drink. "Looks like her training is going exceptionally well. If you need to practice some more, Dani..." He held up the keys to a Lust Room, dangling them in front of me. "I have this."

Eros tensed slightly, eyes flickering from the keys to Lucifer's smirk. A strong whiff of cinnamon rolled off of Eros, and I relaxed further into the booth. I hadn't even sipped my drink yet, and I already felt drunk off passion.

"Maybe later," Eros said. "What'd you want to talk to us about?"

Lucifer paused for a long moment, gazing around the room at some Wraths making a fuss with the asshole waiter from a few weeks ago. "Dani has gotten herself in some trouble."

14

DEMONIC DESIRES

My brows furrowed. "What kind of trouble?"

"The kind that lands you in the pits of Tartarus, right next to your little boy-toy Javier."

Eros growled and tensed beside me, fingers curling into my shoulder. Javier... I swallowed hard. Don't think about him, Dani. Don't even...

"What kind of trouble?" I asked again.

"Sathanus wants to put a bounty on your head," he said. "Told his son he wanted your horns to hang above the pits so nobody"—He pointed at me—"and I quote 'So nobody takes my fuckin' heirs again.'"

My heart sunk. The Lusts from Chastion this morning were right. Sathanus was out to get me for killing his son. I sipped my drink, trying to stay calm. "What does that mean? What will he do?"

"He tortures people, mostly physically, sometimes mentally." Eros leaned back in the seat, brushing a hand over his face. "Fuck... I should've killed Javier myself. You've put yourself in danger by taking his soul."

"She can handle herself," Lucifer said. "His weakness is the hilt of his tail. If he comes close to you, grab it hard and give it a good whack." He winked. "And tell him that Luci taught you, just for good measure."

I playfully rolled my eyes to show that Sathanus's threat didn't bother me, but it did. Hell, it terrified me because Dad had outlined in his journal all the ways Wraths torture and kill people... and I didn't think I'd enjoy any single one of them.

"What do we do if he threatens her?" Eros asked.

"He won't touch her," Lucifer said.

"What makes you so sure?"

"Because he has a kingdom to lead, and Dani just killed his oldest and strongest heir... He'll get someone else to do his dirty work... He always does."

"Sathanus has other children?" I asked. The thought had

completely passed through my mind these past two weeks. Everything with this ceremony had been keeping me too busy to sit back and think for the shortest moment. I should've known he had other heirs who'd be out to get me.

Luci nodded his head. "Biast Sathanus, the next in line."

I took a long gulp of my Passion Delight until I had drunk the very last of it. Well, fuck. First, I have Javier haunting me... and now I have his brother hunting me. At least, I expected his brother Biast to come at me with revenge.

Eros and Lucifer began talking amongst themselves about the rumors, and my phone started buzzing on the table. Maria's name flashed on the screen along with two texts, asking me where I was.

"I have to go see Maria," I said, scooting out of the booth. "We're helping Trevon move today."

"Trevon? The guy who cheated on you, then got possessed?" Lucifer asked with a smirk. "Don't get yourself into trouble."

I raised a brow at him. "Don't be getting my Eros into trouble, either, Luci." I threw him a wink. "Or I'll come for you next."

CHAPTER 4

"You know you don't have to do this," I said to Maria. I picked up one of Trevon's moving boxes and walked down the hallway with Maria to her grey Audi.

She sighed and pushed the door open, letting her dirty blonde hair fly into her face. "What else am I supposed to do? Live alone?" She gazed back toward his apartment on the third floor, watching Trevon stack box after box in front of the windows. "I hate being alone. These past two weeks have been hell without you."

My lips curled into a soft smile. Though Maria constantly got on my nerves, I missed her and wished that I could've stayed for a bit longer. I shoved the box into the backseat of her car and shut the door. "You could always live in the castle with me and Eros."

Maria broke out into a fit of laughter, her sweet scent filling my nostrils. God, I should've never had that Passion Delight at the Lounge this morning. My gaze flickered to her lips. All my demon could think about was the pure rush I got from taking someone's soul, the feeling of Javier's tense lips becoming soft and lifeless, the adrenaline that pumped through me when I did it.

DESTINY DIESS

I smiled—watching Maria's lips move so effortlessly but not hearing a single word she was saying—and pressed my legs together. No, Dani, you will control yourself. You will not even think about *anyone* the way you think about Eros.

After placing one forearm on the hood of the car and leaning against it, she said, "You know how much I hate demons." She playfully pushed my shoulder. "No offense."

"Offense taken," I said, shaking off any sinful thoughts.

"You know what I mean. And"—She pointed a finger at me —"don't even think about asking me to live with Zane." She gazed down at her phone, frowning. "He's a good time... but... he still wants an open relationship and Dr. U told me I should make sure I'm comfortable with my decision to open up to him before we move forward." And, just for good measure, she added, "And he's a demon too," in case I had forgotten.

I raised a sharp brow. "Well, Trevon was a demon."

"*Was.* He's not anymore." She laughed as we walked back toward the building. "He won't get possessed again. Nobody wants his ass. And, even if he does, you can pop those chains back on him and let him scream for days."

"He's been talking to you about The Chains, too?"

She snorted and pulled the door open. "That's all I hear."

"Well... at least, when he's with you, Zane could watch him," I said. That was the only good thing about this whole arrangement. If Trevon wasn't susceptible to being possessed again, I would *not* let my ex-boyfriend live with my roommate.

"Yeah, that—" Maria stopped completely and stared down the hall with big, bulging eyes. "Is that Samantha?"

My eyes widened as I stared at the petite woman in front of Trevon's door. "What the hell is Samantha doing here?" I asked, my nostrils flaring. A knock-off Gucci purse was hanging off her arm and a stupid smirk was plastered on her face.

Maria's hand tightened into fists, and she said something. But again, I couldn't hear her. All I could focus on was Samantha, her

18

DEMONIC DESIRES

pungent scent, and the hundreds of reasons she could be at Trevon's door.

Trevon leaned one arm against the doorframe and smiled down at her. She ran her fingers across his bicep as if she had done it so many times before. I growled under my breath, trying to hold myself together. I couldn't let my demon take control because she would do something murderous.

What the actual fuck was going on? Trevon fired her because she spiked my drink. Did he not remember? Was he that stupid to let her back into his life? Maybe they were fucking. Maybe he just didn't give a single shit.

She curled her arm around his, pressing her breasts against his chest and batting her fake lashes at him. What was wrong with him, going for someone like her? He could do so much better.

I wasn't jealous of her. I was furious at him.

Five entire years with him, dealing with his ass when he cheated on me, worrying about him nonstop when he was possessed, and he goes back to someone who had tried to poison me?

I cleared my throat, and Trevon gazed over at me, his brown eyes soft and hazy. God, why was he so gullible? Samantha giggled at me. "Dani," she said in her high-pitched, annoying ass voice.

"Samantha," I said, plastering a fake smile on my face and trying my hardest not to gag from her stench. "What are you doing here?"

The greens in her eyes glowed faintly. She ran her manicured fingers against Trevon's chest, and Trevon stiffened. "I just wanted to help Trevon move."

"I'm sure you did." I walked right up to them, grabbed Trevon's hand, and tugged him back into his bare apartment. "Trevon, I need a word with you." I slammed the door in her face and turned on my heel toward him, clenching my jaw.

19

Trevon pulled his arm away from me. "What are you doing?"

"What am *I* doing? What are *you* doing?" I raised my brows at him. "She spiked my drink more than once. You had to *fire* her, if you don't remember." The apartment was completely quiet, and I remembered all the late nights we used to spend here, all the early mornings when he'd make me breakfast, all the smiles and laughs and I still hurt a bit from his betrayal... but I wasn't acting this way because of that. I just wanted to protect him like he protected me when we were younger. "You shouldn't be seeing her."

"It's in the past. I know she fucked up big time, but she's different now." He gazed at the closed door and... smiled? "Why're you freaking out about this? We're not dating anymore, unless... unless you want to."

"We're not dating anymore," I said. "And we won't ever date again... but that doesn't mean I don't care about you. I don't want someone who will scheme and hurt others to get what she wants to influence you." I grabbed his hands, holding them close to me, and my heart tightened. "You're healthy now and you need to stay strong."

Because I wouldn't be able to deal with him turning into a demon again, especially not emotionally. When I saw Trevon for the first time after they released him from The Chains, my heart shattered into a million pieces. Nearly skin and bones, he had lost most of his muscle. He still had the two scars shooting out from either side of his lips from where the demon ripped right through him.

Lucifer's healers helped him a lot, but they couldn't help me from unseeing how my strong ex-boyfriend had turned into a monster, then into nothingness.

I didn't want to lose him like I had lost Kasey, Aarav, and Mycah as friends. I couldn't bear to lose another friend, especially to someone who didn't deserve him. But I wanted him to be happy or, at least, try to lead a normal life again.

DEMONIC DESIRES

My fingers relaxed on his wrists. "Just be careful with her and don't take her over to Maria's house." I smiled. "Maria would put a mascara stick right through her throat for what she did to me, if she showed up at the apartment."

He chuckled. "I wouldn't do that to Maria." Suddenly, he got all quiet and stared at me with a lightness in his eyes. He brushed his knuckles against my cheek. "You don't have to worry about me, Dani," he said quietly. "Javier is gone. You took care of him, didn't you?"

I sucked in a deep breath and nodded my head. "I did."

He clutched the cross on his neck, thumb brushing against the shiny golden metal. "Thank you. Thank you so much for everything." His eyes softened even more, and I relaxed further. Something about him seemed off—not in a bad way but in a way that reminded me of Mom, of softness, and of care.

His gaze flickered to my lips. And that's when I saw that same desire in his eyes that Eros had given me so many times before. I tensed and backed away from him, knowing what was coming next. "I should be going. We can't fit anymore boxes into Maria's car." I grasped the door handle, but Trevon caught my wrist and tugged me back.

"Do you want to go out sometime?" he asked me. My eyes widened. Out? As in on a date? Didn't he know that I was with Eros still? His lips curled into a smile. "Not as boyfriend and girlfriend, just as friends. We didn't make it to the nursing home this year together. I thought that maybe you'd like to go."

"Um..." I took a deep breath. Maybe this would be good. Maybe grounding myself back on Earth would help me relax a bit during all the drama in Hell and help me find myself again. I nodded my head. "Sure."

CHAPTER 5

"How was your trip to Earth, Commander?" Esha asked in Lust's portal room. She stood from one of the velvet couches and bowed her head, handing me a glass of Passion Delight.

I handed it back to her, raising my brow. "Did Eros ask you to give me this?"

She blushed softly and nodded her head. "I shall tell him you arrived."

"He already knows," I said, walking out of the building and staring into the dark maroon sky. "You're free for the rest of the night, Esha. Go enjoy yourself."

After she parted ways with me to head to Chastion, I made a bee-line toward the castle. Lusts were still whispering about my crowning, and I didn't have the energy to confront them for it. All I wanted was to lie in Eros's arms and relax tonight.

Sathanus, Javier, and Samantha had been on my mind since I left Earth, haunting me like a fucking nightmare. I stepped into the house and walked up the hundreds of stairs to our bedroom. If I could—

"Dani, Dani, Dani…" Eros shut the bedroom door, as if he had been waiting for me, and shook his head. Eyes full of sin, full lips parted in pure delight, an alluring scent of cinnamon apple, he stepped closer to me and stared into my eyes.

I swallowed hard, completely entranced by his beautiful black orbs. They showed me every single one of his wants: to lock me in our bedroom, to pick me off the ground, to tug onto my hair and thrust himself deep down my throat. Every single one... crawling into my mind, fusing into every particle of my being, becoming *my* desires.

He curled a finger around a strand of my hair, pulling on it softly, and inhaled. "Why do you smell like Trevon?" he asked, his voice a domineering kind of tense. He grasped my horn, tugging my head to the side and placing his mouth on my exposed jaw. "His scent is all over you." He drew his nose up the column of my neck, lips brushing against my skin.

I shivered from his touch, my toes curling. "I could ask the same thing about Lucifer."

"You're mine, Dani." His hand snaked around my throat, and he squeezed lightly. "Mine to bend over our bed." He spun me around and placed a hand on my back, pushing my chest onto the bed. His fingers curled around my hips. "Mine to touch." He plunged his hand into my jeans, rubbing them harshly against my panties. "Mine to make cum when I want you to cum."

I grasped onto his wrist, arching my back and pressing my ass against his hardness. His fingers moved in quick circles around my clit, making me clench. Heat warmed my core, and I closed my eyes. "Eros, don't stop." His fingers moved even quicker, pressure building in my core. "Eros... Eros... I'm going to—"

He pulled his fingers off my core, and I whimpered. "Don't do this..." I tugged his wrist toward my clit, yet he didn't move.

Instead, he grasped a fistful of my hair and pulled me closer to him, his lips against my ear, those tortuous fingers just hovering over my clit and teasing me. "I do what I want with you, Dani." He chuckled deeply into my ear. "You should know this by now."

He turned me around to face him, wrapped his hand around my throat, and thrust his finger into me.

My demon stirred, begging for me to kiss him. Just one taste, that's all she wanted. We weren't that greedy. We could hold back from taking all of his soul. My heart raced, and I watched his lips part. Unless he tasted too good, then we wouldn't be able to control ourselves, then we'd take all of him and savor every single...

Eros pushed my head to the side and stepped closer to me, pressing his cock against my stomach and letting me feel it grow. God, it was so big, so damn big. He ran his nose up the side of my neck. Pure ecstasy ran through my veins, every time he'd pull his fingers away and waited for me to settle back down.

We could've been there for hours—I didn't know, nor did I care. The scent of cinnamon and Delights and apples was enough to keep me teetering on the edge. Nothing could ruin this moment...

But then he brushed his fangs against the crook of my neck, and I gasped, my eyes shooting open. All I could see was fire, lava, a kingdom of ash and of heat and of... Javier standing in front of me with those sinful maroon eyes that made me want to devour him all over again. I would be lying if I said that I didn't want to taste his lips, to taste his licorice and his wrath again.

I slammed my hands hard into Javier's chest, my vision slowly starting to come back to me. Instead of Javier stumbling back, Eros did, his brows drawn up in confusion and in fear. He placed his hands on my forearms, trying to calm me down.

"Dani," he whispered, all his lust disappearing. "Are you okay?"

After shaking my head to rid myself of that damn disgusting man, I inhaled Eros's cinnamon, my body relaxing.

Cinnamon. Cinnamon. Cinnamon. I loved Eros and his cinnamon.

You enjoy my licorice too, Dani," Javier said in my mind.

I shrieked and shook my head. No. No. No. He wasn't really there. He couldn't be. Javier was dead. Javier was long gone. I killed him. I was sure of it. I cut off his horns, as Eros told me to do, and sent him off into the pits of Tartarus so he would burn for eternity.

Eros wrapped his arms around my body and pulled me closer to him. "Dani," he murmured against my neck. He grasped my hand and placed it over my parents' ring. I rubbed the cool, smooth texture, and took a deep breath. "It's me... Eros." He paused for a moment. "You're okay, Dani. It's me."

He parted his lips to say something else, then pushed them back together. A moment passed, then two, and I had the urge to blurt out every single thing that had happened since this morning, but I didn't.

How would Eros react to me dreaming about his brother?

Horribly.

Thanks to his parents constantly putting him down and making him seem as if he wasn't a true incubus... he already felt like he wasn't good enough. What would he think when he compared my dreams of him to my dreams of his brother?

I parted my lips, unable to get any words from coming out of my mouth.

"What just happened?" Eros asked, pulling away from me. "You had that same look on your face you had when you killed Javier, that same look of... insatiable desire."

My eyes widened. "No," I said, shaking my head. I did *not* desire a dead man and I did not desire his brother. Ever. I hated Javier for what he did to Trevon, almost as much as Eros hated him. I shook my head again, trying to convince myself that what I was thinking was true. "Nothing's wrong. I'm just..." I took a deep breath, my shoulders rolling forward. "I'm just stressed out about everything. Sathanus. Biast." *Javier.* "Trevon and Maria. Being crowned commander." I gazed up into his eyes. "What if... what if Lust doesn't accept me?"

DESTINY DIESS

Eros lips turned into a frown for a split moment. "Lust already loves you because of your father."

"But I'm not my father," I said. "I'm a half-angel, half-demon hybrid leading one of the most powerful kingdoms in Hell. What if everyone thinks I'm not fit to rule?"

He ran his fingers through my hair, near my horns, and made me hum in delight. "You'll be fine, Dani. Nobody will find out about you. I will make sure of it." He pressed his lips to my forehead. "Tomorrow we meet with the other commanders to officially announce your crowning and then we'll continue your training."

My eyes widened. "Other commanders? Even Sathanus?"

"He won't hurt you. If he comes within five feet of you, I'll have his throat."

I hesitated but then nodded my head. Eros would protect me. He protected me from all the darkness so far, he will protect me with this too. But... he couldn't protect me from the demon inside me, and he couldn't protect me from the truth.

Eros tugged on my hand. "Let's go lie down."

"I'll go to bed soon." I pulled my hand away from his and smiled. "I want to go read Dad's journal to clear my mind." I paused for a moment when his eyes flashed a deeper black. "I promise that I'll be back up."

After pressing my lips to his, I walked to Dad's office. I hadn't had much time to read through our family journal yet, but I had taken it from the library and locked it in his desk. I sunk into Dad's chair and pulled it out.

A thick layer of dust covered the maroon leather binding. I took off my ring and stuck Mom's pendant into the heart-shaped key slot. With a low click, the book unlocked. After putting the ring back onto my finger, I blew out a deep breath.

Part of me wanted to go upstairs with Eros and worry about this journal tomorrow, but I couldn't. I didn't want to dream of Javier again and I didn't want to daydream of him either.

DEMONIC DESIRES

Once I opened the book, I aimlessly skipped through the first few pages. I should probably talk to someone like Dr. U had always suggested, but who could I talk to? Not Eros. Not Trevon. Not Kasey. Not Luci. Maria didn't like talking about Javier, so she was out of the question. The only people I had down here were Mom and Dad... I drew my thumb over my ring... and they weren't even here.

After shuffling through some pages of Dad's journal, I stopped at one labeled *Beliel's Prophecy*. Unlike all the other pages, this page had been torn out of another journal and stuffed into this one. The off-white paper felt brittle, the handwriting a strong cursive.

Beliel's Prophecy
Beliel, the first angel to have her wings seared off by God, fell from the Heavens above. Though nobody ever saw her again, she carved her prophecy into a stone in Wrath, claiming to have seen the future as the first fallen angel.
The stone reads:
Three demons will rise from the ashes:
The Devil, The Beast, The False Prophet.
God will call them the Triad of Sinners,
We will call them the Unholy Trinity.
Under them, Hell will rule the Earths,
And Heaven will fall to ruin.

And, as soon as I read those words, my stress went through the damn roof. Being a Commander was more than I bargained for.

CHAPTER 6

I stepped onto solid Earth through the portal near The Lounge and gazed around the empty alleyway to make sure nobody had seen me. A thin layer of snow covered the cement. I walked toward the back entrance and banged on the door with the side of my fist.

Someone glanced through the peephole and opened the door. "Commander," the burly man said. "Your usual?" When I nodded my head, he disappeared down the hallway.

A breeze hit my exposed legs, and I wrapped my arms around myself. The city was quiet this morning, the usual morning crowd wouldn't show up for at least another hour. I yawned, the cold keeping me awake. I didn't sleep at all last night. Hell, I didn't even leave Dad's office.

Instead, I continued to read through his journal, an uneasy feeling sitting heavily in my stomach. Whoever the Devil, the Beast, and the False Prophet were... Dad said that they were three unconquerable fiends, each with an uncontrollable rage inside of them and an unquenchable thirst for death, destruction, and domination.

The burly man reappeared with a bag of Fervor Crisps and

leaned against the door. "Here you go, Commander." His gaze flickered lower for only a moment, and I grabbed the bag from him. Trying not to breathe in his scent or the scent of the others down in the Lounge.

"Thanks," I said, hurrying down the alleyway toward Ollie's.

Something in my gut told me that once these three demons rose, The End would begin, and that time was *soon*. My kingdom would not fall to these demons; we would rise above them. Eros and I would hold the kingdom together, just like I needed to hold myself together when I was around literally anyone who smelt good. My demon stirred inside of me.

When I arrived at Ollie's, I smiled at the hostess. "Just tea with honey to-go," I said. As she poured the boiling water into a styrofoam cup, I gazed around the restaurant to look for Mycah. The hostess handed me the cup, and I leaned over the counter. "Is Mycah here?"

She frowned at me. "No. She took a couple weeks off."

I nodded and walked back out toward Dr. U's building. God, I wanted to go over to Kasey's so badly, but she changed her entrance code to get into her building. She hadn't answered any of my calls. She had been ignoring me far harder than Eros had ever ignored me. She didn't even want to talk about what Eros did to their parents.

Once I entered Dr. U's building, I shook the snow off my sweater and walked toward her office. I knocked twice and peaked my head into the room. She shuffled through some papers and gazed up at me. "Dani!" she said, her eyes widening. She brushed her chocolate brown hair over her shoulder. "I wasn't expecting to see you here today."

I placed the Fervor Crisps and Ollie's tea down on her desk. "I come here almost every day, Dr. U."

She arched a brow and sipped her tea, staring at me from across her mahogany desk. "Not this early... and especially not with you looking..."

29

DESTINY DIESS

My lips curled into a smile. "Do I look that bad?"

"You don't look bad, Dani. You've just never been this... tired, since you've been with Eros." She furrowed her brows like she always did when talking to her clients and took off her glasses. "Something's wrong."

I licked my lips and glanced through the window overlooking the city. Tiny little snowflakes drifted down from the sky, and I inhaled the scent of Fervor Crisps. Was there something wrong? No, of course not. I was just having dreams of my boyfriend's brother; I was worried about the Crowning Ceremony; and now I had to deal with this Unholy Trinity.

But there was no way I could tell Dr. U about this because I hadn't told her about Hell. Sure, she knew something had happened and she might've had her suspicions... but I didn't want her to get involved.

She grabbed my hands from across the table and squeezed tightly. Mom's lightness fluttered in her eyes, and I brushed my fingers against my ring. She smiled down at it. "You can tell me, Dani. I'm not gonna tell anyone and I'm not gonna judge you."

After glancing back at the closed door, I took a deep breath. "I've been... having these dreams, like the ones I had of Eros a few weeks ago."

"I don't see anything wrong with that. You're not dating Trevon anymore, and Eros *is* your boyfriend." She furrowed her brows together as if she didn't understand my concern.

"The dreams..." Oh, god, how do I say this? "The dreams aren't of Eros." I clenched my hands into fists, trying not to let my thoughts of Javier drift freely through my mind. "They're of Eros's brother."

She choked on her tea and squeezed my hand tighter. "What do you mean they're of his brother?"

"I mean that I have been having these really weird visions of him..." ... sexual visions. "Usually when I'm with Eros or when I should be with Eros."

30

"Have you seen him a lot lately?"

I shook my head. No, I hadn't seen him because he was dead. I killed him with my bare hands and my lips, sucked his soul right out of his body, drank it up, inhaled him, touched him. All I wanted was to feel that power between my lips again.

"Dani," Dr. U said, wiggling her hand in my grip.

My eyes widened as I stared at the red marks I left on her fragile hand from how tightly my fingers were wrapped around it. I pressed my lips together and sat on my hands, so I couldn't do that again. Dani, breathe. You can't lose control like Trevon did.

"Sorry," I whispered.

Dr. U sat back in her seat and rubbed her wrist. "Do you miss him?" She paused for a long moment, eyeing me. "Or are you not telling me the whole story?"

I ached to tell her about what happened with Javier. But if I told Dr. U about me killing someone, what would she think of me? Would she turn me into the police? Would she understand if I told her I did it with my own lips? What would she say to me about it? That it was just my guilty conscience getting the best of me?

If I had a guilty conscience, I wouldn't be dreaming of him touching me like he did. I would have had nightmares of slaughtering him over and over again. Not of these intimate visions and voices.

My phone buzzed in my pocket, and I glanced at the clock on the wall, reading *7am*. The meeting with the other commanders was in less than an hour. Even if I wanted to tell her, I didn't have time. "Sorry, Dr. U." I shot up from my seat and hurried to the door. "I have to go."

CHAPTER 7

When I returned to Lust, Eros waited on the palace stairs for me. The wind blew his soft brown hair into his face, and all I wanted to do was run my fingers through it. But before I could, he grasped my hand. "We have a meeting with the commanders in five minutes. Where have you been?"

Our guards opened the palace doors for us. We walked into the large foyer decorated with six chandeliers. I stared down at my feet, watching the stone floors underneath them. "I was just talking to Dr. U."

"On Sunday morning?" he asked, his voice tense. "Why'd you need to see her today?"

After shrugging my shoulders and responding with a curt *"No particular reason,"*—even though there was definitely a particular reason—I followed Eros into the meeting room.

The ceilings were tall, the walls an eggshell-color. I rubbed my sweaty palms together and gazed at the other six commanders waiting for me at the long mahogany table in the center of the room. Hell's finest nude mosaics from each of the kingdoms adorned the walls.

Lucifer sat at one head of the table with his horns of ice tilted away from Sathanus and his chilling gaze focused on me. The Greed Queen sat to his left, dressed in the shiniest diamonds and a blue silk dress. The Envy with the piercing green eyes sat next to her, glaring at the table in front of her. Sathanus was at the other head of the table, eyes a blazing red and tail curled tightly around a leg of his chair. And then there was the Sloth and Glutton Princes, both smoking a blunt, munching on Glutton Tarte, and not giving a single fuck that they'd been summoned to a meeting.

I stopped at the door, trying to gather my thoughts. With all the information thrown at me lately, I couldn't think straight, nevermind announce to the six other commanders of Hell that I would be the next queen when I didn't know the first thing about leading people.

Eros brushed his fingers against my lower back, ushering me toward the table. I sat next to Lucifer, my palms sweating. His lips curled into a small, sinful smirk.

Sathanus glared at me, his fiery gaze making me hot. I tried to not look in his direction because all he did was remind me of Javier... and I didn't need him distracting me at the moment.

I smiled at the other commanders and was met with no greeting back. Instead, the Greed Queen looked me up and down, clearly not impressed by the lacking number of jewels on my body. "This will be the new commander of Lust?" She arched a hard brow. "She is Asmodeus's child?"

Lucifer cocked a brow. "She is."

Envy rolled her eyes. "She barely looks like she could handle one of you, nevermind the entire kingdom. How could someone like her... control Lust? She looks... virtuous."

"Virtuous? The first night she met me she had my cock inside her. She's no angel..." Lucifer said, but there was a lightness to his words. Only he and Eros knew I was part angel, and I planned to keep it that way for now. Lucifer sipped his Vemon, a traditional Pride drink. "Isn't that right, Dani?"

33

DESTINY DIESS

I swallowed hard, hoping to keep myself calm. "Yes," I said, cheeks turning red.

"Oh, come on, Lucifer. She's embarrassed by the mere thought of it."

Lucifer leaned back in his seat. "You should be afraid of her, Akoda." He swirled his drink in his hand. "She's stronger than you ever will be." His gaze flickered across the table. "Sathanus knows that, don't you brother?"

Sathanus growled and slammed his fist on the table, making it shake. He leaned over it, stared right at me with his burning red eyes, and curled his tail around the leg of my chair, pulling me closer to Sloth. "You're the one who killed my heir. Your entire kingdom will pay for your mistakes."

Though fear ran straight through my bones, I wasn't going to give him the satisfaction of seeing me scared. Instead, I did what any Lust would do: sat up, pushed my chest out, and gave him the same smirk I had given his son before I killed him. "I will become commander, Sathanus."

He narrowed his gaze, fire forming on his fingertips.

Don't let your voice waver, Dani. Don't show him your terror. He feeds off of it.

"I am the daughter of Asmodeus. I am the best fit as the new ruler."

But... I wasn't sure I believed it myself.

Envy flicked her chipped nails at me. "How do we even know you're telling the truth? Who is your mother?"

My mother? She wanted to know who Mom was? I couldn't tell them. I had to keep it a secret. If I told them Mom was an angel, they'd throw me straight out of Hell, would refuse to acknowledge my claim to the throne, and would spew lies about me to everyone.

I slid my ring off my finger under the table so they couldn't see my parents' wedding band. "Does it matter who my mother was? My father was Asmodeus."

34

DEMONIC DESIRES

"Probably one of the Lust whores," Envy said to Greed.

Sloth looked at me and shook his head at the other commanders. "Why does it matter who she is?" He raised his brow, his bloodshot eyes looking me up and down. "She's hot." He took another hit of his blunt. "Come to Sloth, and we can chill sometime."

Envy rolled her eyes. "I don't think somebody who might not even be related to Asmodeus should wear the crown. And even if she is related to him, he was a traitor. He went against his kingdom to marry an angel." Envy looked at me with glowing green eyes. "She will be a traitor too."

Sathanus growled again. "A traitor and a killer. Somebody who's willing to kill the heir to the throne of Lust and the throne of Wrath."

Eros clenched his jaw and stepped forward, staring right at Satan. "Your son was not heir to the throne. Biast will become your heir. Dani didn't kill anyone who didn't deserve to die."

Lucifer sat back in his seat, humming to himself. I cut my eyes to him. "Dani, Dani, Dani, always causing trouble, aren't you?" He smiled and shook his head.

I ignored him and turned back to the commanders. Greed set up taller and pressed her lips together. "For what it's worth, I don't care who you are. Just don't get in my way from taking it all."

Envy flared her nostrils, and I pressed my lips harder together. Something inside of me wanted to show everyone right then and there that I was the true heir to the throne, that I could take their lives with a single kiss, that I—Stay calm, calm, calm, Dani. Don't lose to the darkness inside of you.

Sathanus looked at me with eyes so similar to Javier's, and I remembered everything that he had told me in my dream. That his kingdom would be mine and my kingdom would be his... That when I was crowded, we'd rule together... That... Stop.

35

DESTINY DIESS

He wasn't here. He wasn't real. He was dead. Dead. Dead. Dead.

"She is not heir to the throne. She doesn't deserve it. One of my sisters should have it," Envy continued, tossing her hair over her shoulder. "Maybe I should take it for myself."

The darkness clawed its way up inside of me again, and an insatiable hunger appeared in the pit of my stomach. My demon ached to feed off of her, to learn how envy would taste on my tongue.

"I will become the Commander of Lust and if you stand in my way..." I stared right at her. "I'll feed off you the same way I fed off Javier. With my hand around your throat, with lust pumping through my veins, and without mercy when you're begging me to stop."

Sathanus slammed his palms onto the table and postured over it, trying to intimidate me. But the darkness in me took total control of my body, and I mirrored his movements. I might've been smaller than him, but I was more deadly.

His tail wrapped harshly around my neck, and I gasped. It had come so suddenly that I didn't have time to think about how a true commander should react to another commander's threats. So, instead of killing him like I had killed his son, I grabbed his barbed tail in my fist and tugged on it—desperate for air.

"You will fucking pay for this." Sathanus seethed. Eros growled and stepped forward, but I yanked Sathanus's tail off of my neck before Eros could do anything else and then I glared right at Sathanus. "My son, Biast, will kill you and rule over all the kingdoms."

CHAPTER 8

After the meeting, I hurried to the Throne Room and rubbed my throat. I could feel Sathanus's tail burning into the skin, just like I could feel Javier's fangs on my neck from the other night. What the hell did I just do? Talk back to Sathanus, one of the most powerful, wrathful men in all of Hell? That would lead me straight to the Pits of Tartarus before I could even be crowned.

I closed the door, breathing deeply, and stepped onto the red carpet which led directly to the throne. If I didn't get this Javier thing under control and stop lying to Dr. U and finally tell Samantha to stay the fuck away from one of my friends, I would lose control and Sathanus would grind me up into tiny little pieces and scatter my organs all around Wrath.

The door opened behind me, and cinnamon drifted in through my nose. "Dani," Eros said. I listened to him walk closer and closer, his steps soft on the carpet. My arms wrapped around me, and I suddenly felt like I was slipping out of control.

What if one night I end up losing it and killing Eros? What if I couldn't control my lust, my need, my hunger to kiss someone, to

DESTINY DIESS

suck their life essence between my lips, to watch them fall to their feet in front of me?

Eros wrapped his arms around my waist, his lips pressed against my ear, his shirt faintly smelling like apples. "Don't let Sathanus get inside your head," he said. But it wasn't Sathanus that I was worried about getting inside my head.

It was Javier.

He nodded toward the throne. "You belong here, Dani. No matter what anyone ever says. You belong right on this throne." He picked me up, and I wrapped my legs around his torso, holding him to me tightly.

I was scared. Scratch that, I was terrified that this would end all before it could even begin. I was terrified that I'd let down Mom and Dad. They had died for me to stay alive; I couldn't honor them if I was dead too.

Eros placed me down on the velvet throne, his lips traveling from my lips to my jaw to my neck. "You belong as my Lust Queen," he whispered into my ear. I shivered at his voice, the sweet melody bringing me back to the first day I met him. He brushed a finger against my ring, and I brushed my fingertips against his forehead, pushing some strands of his dark hair from his face.

The door opened behind Eros, and I watched Lucifer enter. He leaned against the door, icy eyes trained on me. "Looks like your demon is finally giving you a backbone, Dani."

Eros sat on the side of my throne, trailed his fingers up the insides of my thigh until they pressed against my core, and glanced at Lucifer. Lucifer's eyes dropped down my body for the slightest moment to his fingers.

"Leave us, Lucifer," I said.

"Someone's touchy this morning." He smirked, turned back around, and threw his hand into the air. "Well, I'll be in Pride if you need me." Before he shut the door, he gazed back at Eros. "Don't disappoint her, Eros."

DEMONIC DESIRES

When the door closed, I raised a brow at him. "Does he think he's going to get another threesome?" I asked. "Because I am *not* doing that again."

Hell, I wanted to... but I promised Eros that it'd be us until we got this kingdom under control, and I planned on sticking with that, especially now that I kept thinking of Javier.

Eros's lips curled into a smirk. "You seemed to like it last time."

"Last time was different."

He arched a brow, his fingers moving in harsh, little circles through my panties. "How was it different? You felt good, didn't you?" He pressed his lips to my jaw, his cinnamon scent making me shiver. He curled a hand around my throat and pulled me closer to him. "Your preparations *officially* start today, Dani. How should we start?"

He curled a finger around my bra strap, then released it harshly. "By taking this off?" He slipped his other fingers inside my panties. "Or these."

My mind buzzed with excitement; lust pumped through my veins. He pressed two fingers into me and his eyes flashed maroon for a moment. Just like Javier's.

God, no, not again. I swallowed hard. It's all fake. It's all fake. It's all fake.

Eros chuckled in my ear. "Your pussy just got so wet," he said.

Damn it.

I closed my eyes again. He wasn't here. Javier wasn't here.

Eros's fingers pumped slowly in and out of me, and when I reopened my eyes, the black eyes that I fell in love with stared down at me. Eros pushed his fingers into me again, his thumb massaging my clit.

I threw my head back against the throne, digging my fingers into the plush velvet. "Eros... I'm going to..."

He pulled his fingers away from me, just before I came, chuckling menacingly in my ear. Tingles shot up and down my arms and legs from his mere laugh. I felt like I was lying on the pink feathery clouds of Lust, being devoured by a higher being, a god, a demon.

For minutes, if not hours, he teased me, getting me to the very edge but refusing to give me such a simple pleasure. He placed his lips all over my body, worshiping me. I rested my hand on his cock through his pants, stroking him gently.

"Eros..."

"Beg for it, Dani."

"Please."

"Louder."

"Please."

He grasped my jaw in his hand, forced me to look up at him, then rested his forehead against mine and closed his eyes. When his forehead touched my own, my mind raced with a hundred thousand visions of us. I walked through Eros's thoughts, staring at all his deepest, darkest desires.

Me on the bus. Me in the car. Me in Lust on this throne.

Him grasping my horns, letting me ride him, fucking me senseless.

When the images stopped, we suddenly appeared in Trevon's bar, Elysium Taproom. Sitting at the wrap-around bar in the back, the dim white accent lights glowing against my thighs, Eros wrapped his arms around my stomach and let me sit on his lap. His cock was buried deep inside my pussy as everyone drank and talked around us.

The bright lights, the smooth texture of the finished wooden bar, the stench of alcohol... it felt so real, like we were really there. But we were only in Eros's mind.

I grasped onto Eros's wrist, digging my claws into his skin. He trailed his lips up the side of my neck. "Here he comes," he whispered against me.

My brows furrowed. Here who comes? Was someone joining us? Would someone see *us*? Trevon walked out of the hallway, saw us from across the room, smiled, and started our way.

I readjusted myself on Eros, smoothing out my skirt to hide what Eros was doing to me as my heart pounded in my chest. God, this felt too real to be just a mere thought. Eros curled his arm tighter around my stomach, drawing me closer to his hard abdomen. "Settle down, Dani." He thrust up into me slow enough to not draw attention, but I could feel his bulge inside of me, stretching me out, filling me up, claiming me as his.

Trevon appeared at the bar next to me, leaning over it. "Dani..." His gaze traveled to Eros, and he nodded his head. "Eros."

Eros continued to thrust into me, his fingers slipping lower and lower down my stomach. I curled my toes and pressed my lips together, careful not to make a sound.

"Wanna drink?" Trevon asked, hopping over the bar.

"N—"

"She'll do a shot of Vodka," Eros said.

I nodded, wanting him to just leave us. Trevon turned toward the bottles, and Eros gazed up at me and began pounding into me. "I'm going to make you scream, Dani. Right in front of your ex-boyfriend."

I pressed my lips together, keeping my eyes on Trevon and watching him look for the best bottle of Vodka to pour. He grabbed one toward the top, his muscles flexing through his shirt. Eros groped my breast, tugging on my nipple through my bra. Heat warmed my core, and I clenched hard on him—unable to think of anything other than the indescribable pleasure pulsing through me.

Just as I was about to cum, Trevon turned back to us and Eros stopped as if nothing had happened. I grasped the counter, and Trevon furrowed his brows at me. "Are you okay, Dani?"

"Just must be under the weather," Eros said, pushing a strand of hair behind my ear.

DESTINY DIESS

I opened my eyes and pulled my forehead away from him. I gazed around the Throne Room, horny and upset. "Why do you keep doing this to me? I just want to cum."

He pressed his lips to mine, letting them linger. "To teach you control."

CHAPTER 9

*C*ontrol. I blew out a deep breath and slouched on the throne. I had control.

"You need to learn how to control your urges. Most demons learn control when they're young, others... don't and end up screwing people up like Javier did with Trevon." Eros brushed my hair from my face.

Was Javier out of control? Crazy? Would he have ruined me if he, instead of Eros, slept with me? Something inside of me stirred, my demon awakening. Would I have let him?

Eros picked me off the throne, sat on it, and placed me in his lap. "I'm not going to lie to you, Dani. People have been talking and questioning your ability to rule, especially since you're so young."

I brushed my thumb against my ring in my pocket and slid it back onto my finger. "I know..." People were whispering about me around the castle, out in Chastion, everywhere. I had hoped that the rumors would die out soon, but with Sathanus and those Envies instilling fear and lies into my people, they wouldn't just disappear. "How do I gain their trust and loyalty?"

"Go out, talk to some people around Lust, make friends."

Friends. Friends like Kasey. Except... I sucked at making friends. I rather stay in and keep to myself.

"You don't have to go far, just go down to Chastion," Eros said, placing me back onto my feet. He took my hand and walked with me down the red carpet. "Why don't you go get some Fervor Crisps at the bakery, talk to some people, and come home?"

I sighed through my nose, gazing out one of the palace's open windows. The rose sun was setting over the Garden of Passion, the stone walkways buzzing with people going into Chastion for a night of drinking or toward the castle to use our Lust Rooms.

"Okay... I'll go out for a bit." I swallowed nervously, drawing my finger against my ring. "Just to get Fervor Crisps." I placed one longing kiss on Eros's lips and walked toward the palace's doors.

During times like this, when I had to socialize, I really missed Kasey. Hell, I missed Kasey all the time. She would be so outgoing, could talk to anyone. Me, on the other hand, not so much.

Without waiting for my guard Esha to follow me, I hurried down the stairs and started for Chastion. The walk was short and surprisingly chilly, a strong gust from Pride rolling into the city.

Bustling with people, Chastion was surrounded by the Garden of Passion. The highest buildings weren't taller than ten stories, the sidings either a shiny, metallic fuchsia or a soft, bubble-gum pink.

I ran my fingers along the edges of buildings, remembering the city back home, when Maria would drag me out late for ice cream, when Eros pulled me into his arms next to Ollie's Diner, when Trevon and I used to stay late at his bar and come home early in the mornings.

There were enormous groups of demons around me, laughing with each other. Yet, I didn't know the first thing about how to make friends with them. We were so different. They had spent tens, if not hundreds, of years in Lust... and I had barely been here for two weeks.

DEMONIC DESIRES

So, instead of trying to make conversation with any of them, I made a beeline for Annen's Bakery with the neon purple sign out front, flashing *Open to fill all those late night cravings.*

I was sure there was a double-meaning to that, but I didn't want to think about what Annen—the elderly woman with silver grey hair and cute little glasses—really meant by it. She greeted me behind the counter with a big grin. "Oh, there you are. Dani, how are you?"

"I could be better," I said, frowning at her.

"Does the weather have you down? Lust can get pretty cold when the wind is blowing from Pride." She took out a basket and started placing my usual order into it.

I leaned against the counter and sighed. "No, just… stress. Eros wants me to make more friends here because—"

She eyes me through her thick glasses. "Don't say it. I don't want to hear a word more out of you." She pointed a wrinkled finger at me. "You tell that boy Eros to get his little ass down here and help you make friends yourself. He's the one who brought you here to rule."

My body relaxed, and I grabbed the basket from her. "Thanks, Annen. I'll be sure to tell him." I tossed her some *Joss* money—Hell's currency—and smiled.

"You better or I'll march right up to that castle myself, snatch him by the horn, and drag him down here with you." She smiled and waved me off. "Sweet dreams, dear."

"I'll see you tomorrow." I pushed the door open and stared down at my Fervor Crisps, smiling. Well, at least I had Annen as a friend. She was so easy to talk to and so easy to get along with. I just wished that—

Someone bumped into my shoulder, and I dropped the Crisps. Before they could fly all over the place, the demon grabbed them in one hand and shoved them against my chest. "Watch it."

My brows raised in surprise. The Wrath's irritated words

45

DESTINY DIESS

weren't spoken so commonly in Lust where the sweet greetings were the norm. He growled under his breath, yet didn't move. I gazed up into two red, smoky eyes, my breath catching in my throat.

A red tint to his skin. Black claws. Rough, wrinkled horns. And a huge scar that cut straight through his left eyebrow and down his left cheek. Something about him—his eyes—seemed so oddly familiar, yet I couldn't place where I'd seen him. He snarled at me, his gaze slowly drifting down my body.

"You don't have to be rude." I crossed my arms over my chest, holding the bag of Fervor Crisps close. "Have some respect."

In less than a second, he had curled his hand around the front of my throat and pushed me against Annen's Bakery door. "I don't give a fuck about you or your respect," he said. A red, smoky haze drifted from his eyes, his red tail curling around my wrist and pinning it to the door.

I slammed my hands into his chest. The Fervor Crisps fell between us and onto the ground, but I didn't care. If this was how I would earn respect, then so be it.

His lips curled into a smirk, eyes a terrifying mess. "What are you gonna do to me?" He tilted his head, the golden rings on his pointed ears glinting under the moonlight. "Suck me off until you've had your fill?"

My nostrils flared, my demon stirring. Who did this man think he was?

Someone cleared their throat, and I gazed over the demon's shoulder to see a young woman with pretty green eyes. "Hey, dumbass, do you know who you're talking to?" She stared at the man in front of me, brow arched.

The Wrath demon released my wrist, leaned closer to me, and said, "We'll meet again soon, your *highness*." After pushing me out of the way, his tail brushing against my inner thigh, he walked into Annen's bakery and didn't look back.

I glared through the foggy door. Irritable, snappish, resentful,

DEMONIC DESIRES

and definitely not someone I'd hang out with... but he seemed so damn familiar. Who was he?

The woman waved her hand in front of my face, her emerald eyes glowing. "Don't worry about him. All Wraths are annoying as heaven." She extended her hand. "I'm Maeve."

"Dani," I said, placing my hand in hers.

Her hand lingered on mine, lips curling into a smile. "You're gonna be the new Commander, aren't you?"

"I am." My smile widened.

She gazed down at the Fervor Crisps on the ground between us and nodded toward the center of Chastion. "Come on. I know a place where Wraths like him won't be and you can get your fill of Fervor Crisps all night."

I hesitantly gazed back at the castle, the dark clouds sitting softly around it. I looked back at Maeve and nodded my head. "Okay," I said. This was my chance to make a friend, to destress for a few hours, to get out of the castle, and to stop thinking of Javier. "Let's go."

CHAPTER 10

Maeve grabbed my hand and tugged me through the city. I hadn't been here much at night, only a few times on some late-night Fervor Crisp runs with Eros. Hell, we had been too busy with other work to make it down here that much during the day too.

But Chastion looked even more beautiful on the inside than it did on the outside. Roses hung from balconies, their petals decorating the quiet streets. We walked into the square in the city center. Right smack dab in the middle was a building the size of a stadium. People were lined up outside, dressed in mini-skirts and latex dresses.

Instead of waiting at the back of the line, Maeve dragged me to the front. "This is our Commander. She wants to check out the club. Be a dearest, Xiaxio, and let us in." She dragged her manicured fingers against his taut chest, watching him tense.

The man spared one glance at me, bowing his head briefly, and unhooked the black satin VIP ropes. Maeve tugged me up the stairs and into a large club. The room was spacious. Marble floors, a bright pink light shining from the entire back wall, maroon leather couches.

DEMONIC DESIRES

She leaned closer to me, curling her arm around mine. "This is Rebel!" she shouted over the music. "It's like this all-day every-day with people doing business here or just trying to find a good time."

Unlike the Lounge, Rebel had an upbeat atmosphere to it. People were dancing to EDM-like music and drinking and flirting all over the place. And... there was something else that was different. Glass cubicles lined the walls, each small pod having people fucking inside. The pods closest to the entrance had more vanilla-style sex... but each pod after, the people became more and more raunchy. I squinted, trying to see the last few pods, but the room seemed to go on forever; I couldn't get a good view.

"The farther we walk into the room, the kinkier the sex," Maeve said, noticing my gaze.

Each pod was a different themed desire. Any single desire I could think of was there, all out in the open, for anyone to see: school girls bent over their teacher's lap, sex slaves crawling to their masters. Were those actual people in there? Or just... holograms?

I tried to keep my thoughts straight, but with all these scents drifting around the room, I couldn't think at all.

Maeve grabbed my hand, pulling me close. "And do you see that group of guys over there?" She pointed to a leather couch toward the center of the room. Under the dim light, three men sat talking with each other, each with a Passion Delight. Though I couldn't see their faces from this angle, their backs were sculpted like the heavens, each curve visible through their shirts. And those large, curved horns. I inhaled softly. I could even smell their scents from here: peppermint, citrus, and almond. "That's the Triad."

"The Triad?" I asked, staring at them.

One of them glanced in our direction, his piercing black eyes taking me in. Then he nudged the other two who looked

49

DESTINY DIESS

our way. My eyes widened slightly, noticing Zane amongst them.

"They're the three... how do you say it in human... dirtiest men in Lust."

Zane leaned back on the couch, lips against his glass, his eyes a hazy black. I hadn't seen him so drunk before. He'd always been the calm, collected one. Not the flirt. So, him being part of this Triad... was a bit too difficult to believe.

"They're basically the man whores of Hell. Sleep with plenty of women and men. They don't really have a preference for gender, but... be careful around them because they specialize in taken women."

I glanced back at Maeve. "Taken women?" I asked, a giggle escaping my lips. Eros would kill Zane for even thinking about touching me. I closed my eyes for a moment, trying my hardest to picture Zane as a flirt, but ended up laughing even more.

"Hello Ladies," someone said. I opened my eyes to see them all before us, muscles flexed through their shirts, horns pointed down slightly, dark eyes fixed on me. Everyone in Lust was beautiful, but these men were the breathtaking kind.

"Commander," the other one said, voice husky. He had two deep dimples on his cheeks, his blonde hair tousled to one side.

Zane held out two Passion Delights, one for Maeve and one for me. I grabbed one, letting my fingers brush against his. "Dani," he said, lips curled into a seductive smirk. And, it was in that moment, I realized I had never *really* seen Zane flirt. He had said one damn word, and Maeve was already nearly sweating.

"First name basis?" blondie asked, tipping his glass in his direction. "Didn't think you'd had it in you."

Maeve leaned closer to me. "Did I mention that they compete too?" Her lips curled into a smirk. "When they find someone that they like, that is." She wiggled her brows at me, pulling away and gazing back at the guys. "We're here to relax, Axel. Not to talk to guys who can't even perform in bed."

50

DEMONIC DESIRES

Maeve arched a hard brow at Axel, the blonde. He stepped closer to her, grasping her jaw. "Oh, darling, I know you didn't just say that I couldn't perform in bed. I seemed to remember that the last time we saw you... you were begging us to take you."

The two started bickering back and forth, and by bickering I meant flirting. Zane caught my eyes and nodded toward the rear of the room. I pulled my arm out of Maeve's and walked with him and the other man.

"How's Maria?" I asked.

Every time we had taken a step, he had moved just an inch closer to me until his forearm was brushing against mine. Though it was common to walk near each other in Lust, I didn't expect him to do it. And I really didn't expect the hair on my arms to stick right up.

His lips curled into a smirk. "She's... Maria. Me and Enji..." He gestured to the man walking next to us. "... are going to see her tonight."

My brows raised. Damn, Maria. Getting it on with not one but two demons tonight. That girl said she hated demons, but part of me thought that was just her fears. She couldn't resist them.

I sipped my drink and continued walking, keeping quiet. Zane and I never really talked back on Earth, so I didn't really have much to say to him now.

"Are you preparing for the Crowning?" Enji asked, fingers brushing against the center of my back.

"Yes," I said.

His lips curled into a smirk, and he glanced back at Zane. "Good," he said. "We'll be attending. It'll be an enjoyable time, I hope." There was something in his voice that I couldn't quite decipher, a hidden meaning behind his words. And... it kind of scared me. I knew the basics of a Crowning Ceremony... but this Courting Pit was getting me nervous.

"Who are you inviting into your court?" Zane asked.

DESTINY DIESS

"Into my court?" I asked, brows furrowing. An uneasiness feeling washed over me.

"The Courting Pit?" Enji asked, gaze flickering to my breasts. "Do you know what will happen?"

"Of course, I do." I brushed off the comment as if it were nothing and sipped my drink. But I didn't know the first thing about what the fuck I would really have to do if someone challenged me.

"I have to invite people into my court?" I asked Zane, brows furrowed together.

He shrugged. "If someone challenges you, you'll have to prove yourself and you need people to *help* you prove yourself."

I pressed my lips together. Okay, well, I'd think about this later. When I actually wanted to think about what exactly I would be willing to do for the crown. Not when I was in the middle of another sex club.

Maeve finally caught up to us, pulling me away from Zane and Enji. "Time to go. See you later, boys." She tugged me in the opposite direction, a flirty smile on her face. Her neck was painted with red hickies.

I stared wide-eyed at them. "Did you... did you fuck Axel?" God, it had only been a few minutes, and she was just complaining about how much of a man-whore he was.

She blushed and gulped down her Passion Delight. "Maybe." She curled her arm around me and pulled me out the door, heading back through the city. "That's all for tonight. If you stay there for too long—I don't want you to stay there with them for too long. Eros is waiting back at the castle for you, isn't he?"

I nodded my head and walked down the paths with her. The breeze from Pride was strong tonight, and I wished that I had worn more than just this little dress. "Hey, Maeve," I said. "Have you ever been to the Courting Pit?"

She paused. "A long, long time ago. When Eros's mother and father became the new Commanders of Lust."

52

"What was it like?" I asked.

"Well…" She swung our arms back and forth, looking at the Garden of Passion. "All the commanders and everyone from Lust attends the ceremony. It's split into two parts, the Courting Pit and the Crowning Ceremony…" She waved her hand in the air. "The Courting Pit is first… which is where you have to prove yourself worthy of the crown."

I swallowed hard. "And how did Eros's parents do that?"

She stared directly at me, the pink moon bouncing off of her eyes. "They fucked. A lot."

CHAPTER 11

I stumbled back to the palace, my mind buzzing with everything that had happened tonight. Maybe this was what I needed: to get out of my damn head for a bit. Not once had I thought of Javier or all the stress this Crowning Ceremony was giving me or even Trevon's inability to find someone suitable for himself.

The white stone walkways were empty this late. Demons were still in the Palace's Lust Rooms or down in the Chastion or even in the Garden with all the pretty pink flowers that glowed so strongly under the moonlight. My vision blurred for a moment, the Passion Delight suddenly hitting me hard.

My fingers brushed against the roses lining the path as I walked. Part of me worried what Eros would say when I didn't come home with any Fervor Crisps, but he wouldn't mind me getting to know everyone tonight. He'd be proud of me, and that was all I needed to feel good.

Palace guards opened the front doors for me. I grasped onto one of their wrists, leaning closer to him and inhaling his scent. "Where's Eros?" I whispered, wanting to find him and do God-knew-what to him all night long.

DEMONIC DESIRES

After clutching my wrist in his hand, fingers brushing so lightly over my skin, he said, "In his office, Commander."

"And the Lust Rooms?" I asked, my eyes taking in all of him. "Are they *empty?*" He relaxed under my gaze, probably smelling the Passion Delights mixed with the sweet scent of my arousal coming off of me in waves.

I closed my eyes, brushing my fingers against his temple and seeing all of his hidden desires he had buried deep in his mind. Taking me on the castle steps, buried deep inside of me, my hand around his throat, squeezing hard. I shivered and pulled my fingers away.

Eros. God, I needed Eros now.

Without listening to another word he was mumbling, I walked through the open doors and followed Eros's scent. I wandered up the white marble spiral steps toward Eros's office on the second floor.

When I reached the floor, Eros's cinnamon scent mixed with another familiar, lovely one. The moans from the Lust Rooms downstairs drifted up the spacious room, yet all I could hear was the screaming coming from his office.

"How could you do this to her?" someone yelled. It was a woman's voice, filled with anger and hatred and *envy*. My throat dried, my Delight-high quickly fading away. The voice sounded familiar, yet I still couldn't place it. "Do you even understand how much danger you've put Dani in?"

I paused outside of Eros's office door, placing my ear against the wall and listening. Eros walked around the room and sighed softly. "Kasey…"

My eyes widened. Kasey was here? After all this time, she had come back? What was she doing here this late at night? Was this the first time he had seen her since he killed their parents?

"She's stronger than you think she is," Eros said, but I could hear the hesitation in his voice. Kasey knew that I was Asmodeus's daughter, but, like everyone else here, she didn't

55

know that my mother was Fatima—an angel. Everyone thought I was one of the Lust whore's daughters. Not powerful and definitely not worthy of the title *Commander of Lust*.

"Because of your senseless decisions, people are trying to kill her. Rumor has it that Sathanus will have her fucking head." Her voice was filled with so much rage, she almost seemed like a Wrath demon herself.

Eros growled, and I could feel his dominating aura hit me right through these thick walls. I purred softly, the aura arousing me, then I cursed myself for thinking such terrible thoughts at such a terrible time.

He's in the middle of a fight with his sister, Dani. Keep your cool.

But that hunger in me had already been awoken. It was clawing at my insides, begging me to march right into his office and let him take me on his desk. In front of Kasey. Let her watch for the pain she's caused Eros, make her—No. Dani. No. That's Javier talking, not you.

"Sathanus is gathering his army and will march on our kingdom the moment she is crowned."

"Don't envy one of your own fucking friends, someone who'd do anything for you, someone who has been asking about you non-stop and worrying that you won't ever like her again," Eros seethed. Though I had seen him angry before when Trevon turned into a demon, I had never heard him like this. With every word, he raised his voice until he was yelling, until everyone in this entire castle probably heard him.

"I'm not envious of Dani," Kasey said.

"Well, you're acting like Mother did when she wanted to rule Lust," Eros said, distastefully.

"Don't you da—"

Not being able to hold myself back any longer, I pushed Eros's door open and stepped into the heated room. With her hair set in soft, brown waves, Kasey stopped mid-sentence,

DEMONIC DESIRES

dropped her pointed finger at Eros, and looked in my direction. When she had made eye contact with me, her eyes glowed the faintest color green.

They were glimmering, and if I had learned anything here... it was that when Envies envied me, I could see it in their eyes. They glowed with an aura so powerful that I could taste the sourness on my tongue.

Kasey tore her gaze away from me and glared back at Eros. "We will finish this conversation tomorrow."

"There is nothing to finish," Eros said, hardening his stare. He grabbed my hand and pulled me toward him, standing behind me and placing his hands on my shoulders. "Dani will rule our kingdom, whether or not you like it. She's Asmodeus's daughter."

"She's half-human."

My heart skipped a beat. Half-human... sure. That's what I was... not a hybrid.

After giving me a long stare, she clenched her jaw and hurried to the door. I stepped forward, wanting nothing more than for her to stay, to get Passion Delights with me down at the palace bar, to listen to her talk about Aarav and Mycah. I wanted it all back.

God, I was all over the damn place tonight.

"Kasey, wait."

She paused at the door, her chocolate brown curls bouncing on her shoulder. She didn't turn back, and I was suddenly lost for words. What should I have said? That I was glad her mother and father were dead? That they had killed my parents? That... that I only dreamed about all the ways I could've killed them, if I had the chance?

When I didn't say anything, she walked out of the door and down the steps toward the exit of Lust. My heart shattered into a million pieces when I heard the palace doors close.

"I... what's wrong with me?" I asked, curling my arms around myself. Why didn't she want to at least talk to me? Or look me in

57

DESTINY DIESS

the eye? Sure, Maeve would be such a wonderful friend here, but she'd never replace Kasey, the one woman who wanted nothing to do with me anymore. What did I do that was so bad?

Eros tugged me to his chest, his cinnamon enveloping me. I rested my head on his chest, grasping tightly to him. He brushed his fingers through my hair, near my horns, in small circles. "You didn't do anything, Dani." He sighed into my hair, his warm breath making me tingle. "You didn't do anything to her."

CHAPTER 12

*A*fter Kasey left Lust, Eros told me I smelt like hot and angry sex and that he needed a strong drink too cool his nerves. So he had taken my hand, brought me to the portal room, and led me to The Lounge.

Buzzing with more people than usual, The Lounge had humans and demons flirting with each other. On Wednesday nights, this place was open to humans—who innocently thought it was a normal sex club. Unbeknownst to them, they were just lovely succubus and incubus prey.

I sat down in our reserved booth across from Eros. After some detective work on my end, I had found out that these private booths were reserved for the royals in Hell, plus some higher-ranked demons.

A candle flickered between Eros and me, illuminating his striking features. I took a big sip of my Passion Delight and kicked my legs back and forth under the seat. My mind was still buzzing with thoughts of earlier—not only thought of Kasey but of the Courting Pit.

Eros took my hands in his large ones and kissed my knuckles. He closed his eyes, inhaled sharply, and shuddered.

DESTINY DIESS

"What do I smell like?" I asked softly.

He traced the edges of my ring. "Vanilla."

I scrunched my nose, a giggle passing through my lips. "Vanilla?" Way to be basic, Dani.

His full lips curled into a smile, his eyes softening into a lush green. "You might think it's *basic*, but it reminds me of Heaven," he said. The word Heaven rolled off of his lips so quietly that I could barely hear it. It sounded both so foreign yet so familiar on his tongue, like he hadn't said it for ages yet the memories that the word brought back were both good and evil.

Just from hearing the word, some demons looked over at our table. Instead of sparing them a single glance, Eros placed his tattooed forearms on the table and interlocked our fingers together.

"Tell me about Heaven," I said. Mom had always told me bedtime stories about her favorite monsters, but sometimes she spoke about angels. With their grand wings—which were their most sacred possessions—and their glowing white eyes and even the halos that appeared around their heads when they were doing charitable work. Her eyes would become stars, shining so bright that one night four-year-old me had actually asked Mom if she was an angel to which she replied, "I wish I was, Sweetheart..." with eyes full of tears.

At the time, I didn't understand the feeling that had come over her and even now... I was clueless. Why would she lie to me about being an angel? Why didn't she prepare me? Why didn't we live in Heaven?

Eros rubbed soothing circles around the center of my palms. "Heaven was amazing for a long time. We had—we thought we had—everything. All the food and love and warmth we ever needed. We attended church every night; helped the humans down below." He paused for a moment, a warmth that I hadn't seen before crossing his face. "I had the blessing of making some of them fall in love..."

60

"Like a *cupid?*"

"Except without a diaper." He chuckled, then a somber expression replaced his laughter. "It was blissful... until it wasn't enough for some people anymore."

I gnawed on the inside of my cheek, unsure if I should urge him to continue. Mom had told me that some angels questioned God's rule, how some couldn't fathom why God had forbidden the pickings from the Golden Apple Trees or why angels were confined to love one person and one person only, when they had so much love to last a hundred lifetimes over and over.

"What happened?" I whispered.

Eros's lip twitched, eyes turning a shade darker. "A woman named Belial rebelled." After pulling his hand away from me, he grabbed his drink and took a long sip of it. My eyes widened slightly. Belial? That was the woman who prophesied The End from Dad's journal.

The candle flickered between us, crackling softly over the hum of people around us. Eros gazed down at the table, staring into nothingness. "She told Lucifer that there was a world that we would never know about because God kept us confined within the Golden Gates." He took a deep yet shaky breath. "Lucifer listened to her corruption. And then... when she fell, Lucifer followed."

"You were there when it happened?" I asked, watching him nod his head. I sucked in a sharp breath. Dad journal entries were right. Belial had fallen first. I had learned from Mom that Lucifer was the first fallen angel... but maybe she was wrong. "Was my mother there?"

"No, she was born long after I was gone."

All I wanted to do was ask him about his fall, but I didn't want to overstep. Mom hated when I asked her about how good people became bad. She always repelled, as if it was horrific.

"And you?" I asked, testing the waters. He raised his brow at me, so I continued. "How did you fall?"

"I didn't fall."

"You didn't?"

"No." He tilted his head. "When an angel falls from Heaven—at least when I was there—God cuts his or her wings with a transcendental sword She kept around Her neck. My parents cut my wings."

"So... how'd you end up in Hell?"

He stared at me for a long moment, lips pressing together and parting, as if he wanted to tell me but he didn't know what to say. "Belial's fell first." He closed his eyes, jaw clenching like he was reliving some bad memories. "We were in the middle of church... she told God she didn't want to be there anymore. Belial walked right down the center aisle, all the feathers on her wings falling off, and knelt in front of Mother with her back turned. And..." His jaw twitched. "God did as she asked, seared off her wings. Belial fell right through the glass floors and into the darkness.

"Everyone in the church heard the... the... the splat." He shook his head and shivered. "Everyone thought she had died, everyone thought that where she went was the end of an angel's everlasting life."

"But it wasn't..." I said. Belial had written prophecies for the people.

"We didn't know that." He pulled his hands away from me, tucking them under the table. Cinnamon drifted into my nostrils, but Eros wasn't turned on. He was terrified. "Lucifer rebelled next. He walked right up to the altar where Mother stood and told Her to cut his wings, that he no longer wanted to be in Heaven with Her strict rules. Filled with pure rage, Mother cut his wings and he fell. I couldn't let him have the same fate as Belial, so I followed him, caught him in my arms, and let him down in Hell gently."

My lips parted at the pure passion in his voice. Something about the way he talked about Lucifer, the way his eyes lightened by a mere shade, told me he still wasn't telling me everything that had happened in Heaven... but I wouldn't push it.

He had given me more information about Heaven than Mom ever could. And I knew why she had never wanted to talk about it. Eros was saving me the details, and it still sounded so gruesome. But I was thankful that he held back... because... well... I wasn't sure how I'd feel about it.

Mom had two scars on her back, two parallel scars. I remember drawing my fingers against them when I was four, loving to feel the texture of the skin. Her imperfections were so beautiful to me. But... if she was an angel, why'd she have those scars. If my father told her to go up to the Heavens with me, why did we live on Earth with other humans?

I wanted to find out the truth. And, hopefully, one day, when I was prepared, I would.

CHAPTER 13

*E*ros pushed his drink to the center of the table and leaned back. "Enough about me." His dark gaze hardened, and he stared at me with so much mischief in his eyes. "How was Chastion? I heard you went out with some people."

My cheeks flushed, thinking back to all the men and women in those small cubicles, all the dirty things that were doing. I tapped my fingers on my glass. "Chastion was... good. Annen's was better."

"Did you flirt?"

Did I flirt? God, I could barely hold a conversation without stumbling over my words. Flirting was totally out of the question, especially when Eros wasn't with me. If I had to do it—like if another Javier situation popped up out of nowhere—then I would. But... not now.

When I didn't answer him, he raised a brow at me. "Well, if you didn't flirt then, you're going to flirt now." Eros glanced at the pretty waitress behind the bar. She was shaking a cocktail, her breasts bouncing ever so slightly in her tiny little black dress.

My eyes widened, and I shook my head. "No, Eros. I don't even know her name."

DEMONIC DESIRES

"Go ask for her name?" Eros brushed his thumb against my chin. "Get to know her." He paused for a moment. "I'll come with you, if you want."

I gnawed on the inside of my cheek. "You want me... to go flirt with her?" I asked, hesitantly. Don't get me wrong, I knew that he wanted me to enjoy myself with her... but I had never flirted with another woman before and I was more nervous than I thought I'd be.

"Dani," he said. "You need to learn how to control your power. Flirting will help you."

"But... I thought you..."

"Yes, I wanted to keep you only to myself, especially emotion-ally." His lips curled into their signature, sinful smirk. "But I like to watch you flirt." His green eyes faded into black orbs, and I suddenly felt so hot. "You get all flustered."

My pussy clenched.

"Your eyes get wide."

I swallowed hard.

"You don't know what to say so you stumble over your every word..." His voice was low, and he brushed his thumb down my lower lip and inhaled my scent. Then, suddenly, he grasped my chin in his calloused hand. "I can smell you, Dani. I can smell how wet the thought of flirting with her is making you. All those dirty, little thoughts running through your head about the things you could do to her." He shook his head, giving me those *I-can't-wait-to-fuck-you* eyes. "Tell me, Dani. Tell me what you want to do with her."

Every word he said, I tried to deny to myself... but then I gazed over at the bar, watching her lean over the counter, her breasts pressed into it, dark eyes focused on one of the male customers. And my heart was racing.

Maybe it was Eros playing tricks on me, but I swore I saw her glance over at me.

65

"Fine," I said, the warmth in my core growing hotter and hotter. "I'll go over there."

But only because my body felt like it was on fire, only because I needed to prepare myself for this Courting Pit, only because Eros was asking me to. Definitely not any other reason.

As soon as I stood, Eros grabbed my wrist and pulled me into his chest. "You didn't answer me." Cinnamon drifted around us, and I knew that he wanted me to tell him all the desires running through my mind at this very moment. I knew that it got him off. Every time he looked into my mind, he got hard.

"You don't have to ask me to know what I want, Eros," I said, because I wasn't about to admit any of this out loud.

"You know that I'm not going to let you leave without an answer." He slid his fingers from my wrist to my hips, then lower until they hovered over my core. "Now, you're going to willingly answer me, Dani... or I'm going to make you."

Fingers hovering over my clit through my dress, hot breath fanning my neck, dark eyes fixed on me. I parted my lips and stared back over at the waitress who was giving me those sultry eyes again. God, say something. Don't just stand there and—

He pressed his fingers into me, the scent of cinnamon intoxicating me. I grasped onto his shoulder, lips parting wider. "Fine."

"Fine, what?" he asked, fingers moving faster and faster. A wave of pleasure rolled through my entire body, and I could feel the tips of my horns protruding from my head. It was getting harder to breathe, my heart was stammering. He curled a hand around my throat. "Fine, what?" he repeated, dominance dripping from each word.

"Eros," I breathed out, my cheeks flushing. The pressure rose in my core. If he didn't stop, my horns would burst right out in front of all these humans. He slipped his fingers into my underwear, rubbing my swollen clit, feeling my juices on his finger. I was so close to a release, and I knew that as soon as I told him,

DEMONIC DESIRES

he'd let me cum. "Please, Eros... I want... I want to flirt with her. To touch her. Feel how excited she is for me."

"Good girl," he mumbled against my lips. He pulled his fingers away from my clit, smoothed out my dress, and pulled me to him by my throat. "Someone's learning."

I stared at him with wide eyes, my core aching. "You're just going to stop?"

After giving me one of his signature smirks, he took my hand and led me to the bar. I hazily walked after him, my mind buzzing with excitement. Humans and demons alike moved out of our way, letting us sit front and center. Eros slid onto one of the beige stools, and I sat next to him, trying to gather my thoughts before—

"Hi there," the waitress appeared in front of us, her tight black dress hugging her frame perfectly. "Eros... *Dani*... nice to see you again."

I glanced over at Eros, and he watched me curiously. I licked my suddenly dry lips, trying to think about something to say to her. Sure, Asmodeus might've been my father and I might've improved on this whole flirting thing with Eros... but, overall, I sucked at it.

Eros's gaze burned into me, and I kicked my legs back and forth, wishing that he hadn't come over with me. It was... embarrassing, to say the least. Though she had turned me on—and there was no hiding that—I hadn't flirted in front of Eros before with anyone besides with Lucifer.

"Hi." My face flushed a deep red, and I awkwardly smiled at her. Say something, Dani. Don't just sit there and be awkward about it.

"Commander," Eros said to the waitress, squeezing my knee. "She will be crowned as our new commander in less than two weeks."

The waitress's eyes widened, cheeks flushing like mine.

67

DESTINY DIESS

"Commander…" she corrected. She bowed her head. "I'm sorry. I didn't know."

We stayed quiet for a few moments, and Eros nudged me. I could just hear him trying to tell me to flirt in my ear, trying to prepare me for the Courting Pit. But my thoughts were rushing too fast and I couldn't think straight.

"So, um, what's your name?" I asked.

She stared at me with that lustful glint in her eyes and said, "Jasmine… you can call me Jasmine, Commander."

I shifted in my seat. "Nice."

God, I was bad at this.

Someone down the bar called for another drink, and Jasmine hurried over to him. When she turned around, I leaned closer to Eros and sucked in a deep breath. "Can you… um… go sit back down?"

Eros stood faster than I thought he would and walked back to our booth, his scent lingering at the bar for only a moment. He sat back down at our booth and threw me a curious gaze. Well, this was it.

I turned toward the bar and toward Jasmine who was back, standing right in front of me, her chocolate scent filling my nostrils. "Do you enjoy working here?" I asked, awkwardly tapping my fingers on my glass of Passion Delight.

Her full lips curled into a smile. "It pays well, and…" She leaned across the bar, her breasts pressing against it. My gaze flickered down to them for a moment, then back up into her piercing dark eyes. "I got to meet you."

I crossed my legs and leaned forward in my seat, staring into her hazy eyes. "You do this all night, don't you? Find innocent, impressionable people who come into The Lounge and flirt with them until you get what you want."

She brushed her fingers against my forearm, leaning even closer until she was inches away from me. "I haven't gotten what I wanted yet, Commander."

68

DEMONIC DESIRES

Heat warmed my core, and I shifted in my seat, trying to ease the throbbing between my legs. "What if you did?" I asked, testing her. "What would you do with me?"

She paused, gaze flickering to my lips. After brushing her thumb against my bottom lip, she licked hers. "Is that an offer?"

I placed my pointer finger under her chin and lifted it, so she was staring into my eyes. She inhaled sharply, unable to pull her gaze away from me. My lips curled into a soft smile. "Depends on your answer," I said.

Another customer called for Jasmine to come back over to get him a drink, and I took a deep breath when she turned away from me. Her deep brown eyes were still burned into my memory, her scent becoming a part of me.

She walked over to them, her hips swaying back and forth, strands of her curly black hair bouncing on her shoulders. I rubbed my fingertips against the Passion Delight glass. My mind was racing with a thousand different thoughts of her, all of her deepest desires, every single thing that my demon wouldn't mind doing to her.

"She's pretty, Dani." Javier's voice echoed in the back of my mind. I closed my eyes. No, not fucking now, Javier. Get out of my damn mind or, so help me God, I would—"Imagine how pretty she'd look with your hands wrapped around her tiny throat." I snapped my eyes open and saw Jasmine in front of me with wide eyes, flushed cheeks, and my hands around her throat. "Imagine her gasping for air, her mocha cheeks flushed the prettiest color pink, our lips pressed to hers."

When Javier said the word our, I shook my head from side to side, my gaze suddenly refocusing on the empty bar in front of me. Jasmine was pouring a glass of Passion a few feet away, her petite frame unharmed.

God, I needed to talk to Dr. U. Maybe she'd prescribe me some medicine to get rid of these hallucinations because I couldn't be having these... not when I was about to rule this

DESTINY DIESS

kingdom. I needed to be strong for everyone. The End was near.

Jasmine sauntered back over to me, a smile on her lips.

I grabbed my drink and stood, needing to get out of here fast. "Why don't you join the bar staff in Lust Palace?" I said, swallowing all those dirty thoughts Javier was playing inside my mind. "I'd like to see you around more often, *Jasmine*."

CHAPTER 14

When I walked back to the table, Eros was staring at me with hazy green eyes and the smirk that had turned me into a sinner the Sunday morning I met him. "Did you enjoy that?" he asked before biting into a Fervor Crisp.

I slid into the booth next to him, my lips curling into a small smile and my eyes focused on Jasmine. Hell, yes, I enjoyed that. I enjoyed everything until Javier told me to wrap my hand around her throat and to suck her soul from her body. I lo—*hated* that.

He inhaled my scent and slid closer to me. "You loved it," he said against my ear, his finger brushing a strand of hair from my face. "Do you want to know a secret, Dani?" His breath was warm against my neck, making me hot. He grabbed my hand and placed it right on his hardness through his pants. A purr escaped me, my senses sharpening. After brushing his fingers against the inside of my thigh, he said, "I loved watching you, *my little succubus.*"

I clenched. God, how'd he always know exactly what to say and when to say it?

He curled his arm around my shoulders and pulled me to him,

nodding back to the bar. I thought he was nodding to Jasmine, but he had gestured to the far end where Maria, Zane, and Enji were seated.

Zane stood behind a seated Maria, sleeves rolled up his muscular forearms, Passion Delight in one hand. Enji sat in front of her, brushing his fingers against one of her knees. Her cheeks were flushed, plump lips pulled into a smile. Maybe it was my Passion Delight, but even from here, I could smell her arousal.

But it surprised me that she had agreed to come here—out of all places. She knew that The Lounge was a sex-club for demons, and if she hated demons so much...

"What do you think he's saying to her?" Eros asked me, his hand sliding up my bare thigh to my underwear. A wave of pleasure rolled through me, and I pressed my legs together, the high from my Passion Delight hitting me hard.

"Probably the same things that you used to tell me," I teased.

Eros's eyes widened. "Used to?" He pressed his fingers harder into the front of my underwear, rubbing gently through the fabric. "I can still make you cum without even trying, *Dani.*"

"Then why haven't you?" I asked, staring him right in those big, black eyes.

He brushed his nose against mine, sucking my bottom lip between his teeth. "I'm training you."

"Are you sure about that?" I asked, my nipples hardening against my bra. Eros might have known exactly what to say and when to say it, but so did I. *Sometimes.* "Seems like you can't even—"

He wrapped a hand around my throat, pinning me to the beige leather booth. His fangs brushed against my neck. "Are you acting this way because you want me to rip off all your clothes and fuck you senseless in front of all these people, Dani?"

I placed my hand on his thigh, trying to think straight. Warmth pooled between my thighs. Calm, Dani. Stay calm. Don't let Eros know that, yes, you'd definitely like him to fuck you right here in front of all these people. Because... he would.

The mere thought of it was enticing. Hell, the pressure in my core hadn't disappeared since earlier when he was touching me and demanding I tell him all my sinful desires.

"Hmm?" he asked. The candle crackled in the center of the table, yet all I could think about was how strongly the air was charged with cinnamon. So strong. So utterly entrancing. "Because you know that I will."

My toes curled. We had done it in public before on the bus when other demons had pried eyes away from us... but I doubted they'd do that here. They'd probably sit and watch it happen, watch Eros take me, wat—

Eros growled lowly, grabbed my waist, and placed me right on the table in front of him. I gulped nervously and glanced around at everyone. "Eros, wh-what are you—"

He pushed two fingers into me, thrusting them in and out. "Undo the top buttons of your dress."

"We can't do this here!"

Without listening to a word I said, he reached up and undid the top two buttons of my dress for me. Eros didn't care about rules. He did what he wanted, and right now I could see in his eyes that he wanted me. The third button on my dress popped open, my black lacy bra on full display. I grasped his hand before he could undo anymore, my gaze flickering around the bar. Some demons glanced over, yet—as far as I knew—the humans were still preoccupied and so was Maria.

Eros stared at my body, his gaze flickering from breast to breast then to my eyes. "You feel it, Dani?" Eros asked softly, fingers still moving inside of me. "Do you feel everyone staring at you, at their new commander?"

I gulped, my heart pounding in my chest. "Yes. I feel their damn stares." And I wanted to push Eros away because this was embarrassing as hell... but it felt too good. My mind was

DESTINY DIESS

becoming fuzzy, my body was tingling, I felt like I was floating on one of Lust's pink cotton candy-esque clouds.

Classical music played quietly in the bar around us. He curled one hand around my throat, digging his claws lightly into my flesh. "Do you feel their lust?"

I hazily nodded my head. Yes, I felt all of their lust, diffusing off of them, drifting through the air, damaging all of my self-control. I brushed my foot against the front of his pants, feeling his growing cock inside of it.

God, it had been too long since I had craved such an earth-shattering orgasm.

I grasped the edges of the table, my head tingling with cinnamon and all the dirty thoughts that Eros put into my mind. After he pushed his thumb into my mouth, Eros stood and leaned over the table toward me, his fingers plunging into me faster and faster and faster, making me clench.

"You're not going to cum," he said, his voice gruff in my ear, his thumb rubbing circles around my clit. "Not until I give you permission."

"And what if I do?" I asked him, trying so hard to hold off yet teetering so close to having the best orgasm of my entire life.

He squeezed my throat gently. "Cum without my permission, Dani," Eros taunted me. "I dare you."

And while I wanted to cum so damn bad and have him punish me for it, something seemed to hold me back. I knew he'd punish me in a way I wouldn't like. Maybe if we were back home alone, I'd do things differently. But not now.

My legs trembled, and I glanced around the bar. Nobody was staring directly at us anymore, but I could feel the strength of their lust and their arousals hitting me like a wave of pleasure.

"Use their lust," Eros said. "Use it to drive yourself higher, Dani."

I gaze back into Eros's black orbs, unable to pull myself away from them. "Close your eyes." Eros's hand curled around my

DEMONIC DESIRES

throat, squeezing tighter. My eyes fluttered closed. "Breathe it in."

His fingers slowed to a stop inside of me, just pressing against my g-spot. I inhaled slowly, feeling an overwhelming surge in my core. My pussy tightened around Eros's fingers.

"More," Eros said.

My head fell back slightly, and I took another deep breath of cinnamon mixed with other alluring scents. My legs jerked into the air, trembling harder around him. But I held myself together, desperate to cum but desperate to obey him—because if I did, he'd give me what I had been craving for so long.

"Eros," I said in a breathy whisper.

"Again." He tightened his grip around my throat even more, and I took another deep breath. The scents were driving me wild and feral, my horns were so damn close to bursting right through my forehead. "One more."

I took one last deep breath, and Eros placed his hand over my mouth and nose, letting their lust stir inside of me and refusing to let them out. They festered inside of me, building and building, driving me higher, making my core clench even harder on Eros's poor fingers.

"Look at me, Dani."

When I opened my eyes, he curled his fingers in a come-hither motion.They collided with my g-spot, a tsunami of pleasure washing through me. "Cum," he said. My legs shook uncontrollably around him. And I tugged on his hand, needing to pull it away because the pressure was almost unbearably strong.

But he didn't. Instead, he curled his other arm around my waist, took me off of the table, and placed me into his lap. His cock was hard against the front of his pants, and he pushed it against my core. I grasped onto him, my orgasm continuing.

"Next time you cum like this," he said, tilting my head to the side and placing his fangs right on my neck. "My cock will be buried deep inside of you."

I nodded, tugged on his hair near where his horns would be, and whimpered into his neck. "Now. I need it now."

He curled his arms around me, letting me sit fully on him and stared up into my eyes. "No." He lifted his hips higher to press them into mine. "You'll get it when we leave."

"But... but you're teasing me. Please."

He pushed my hair out of my face and pulled my hips down even farther on him. "No."

"Eros," I said, unable to control myself. "Please."

"You've learned to beg," he said, lips curling into a smirk. "I don't even have to train you anymore." His eyes turned another shade darker, and my pussy clenched. His gaze flickered behind me, and he paused. "If you want me to fuck you here, undo my pants."

I narrowed my eyes and looked behind me, watching Maria and Zane walk our way. I playfully slapped his chest and crawled off of him, yet he held me in place.

"Undo my pants," he said more sternly.

"Eros, we can't."

"You either undo them now or I make you undo them when Maria and Zane sit down at this table with us," he said. I growled, the vein in my neck pulsing violently. I grasped his jeans, undid his button, and pulled out his cock. "Good girl." He grasped me and turned me around, so I was facing the table instead of him. "Now, sit."

My eyes widened, and I shivered as his fingers moved up the back of my thighs to lift my dress. He positioned his cock right against my wet entrance and pulled me down onto him, filling me completely.

I closed my eyes, the pressure in my core returning.

"Whoo," Maria said. My eyes snapped open, and I stared in front of us. Maria fanned her face and slid into the booth. Zane sat next to her, grabbing his drink and taking a sip from it, as if he needed something to calm himself down or rile himself up more.

He stared at Eros and I, his eyes lingering on me. My cheeks flushed, remembering earlier when Maeve had told me he was part of the Triad. Eros wrapped one arm around my waist, rubbing my clit under the table, and grabbed his drink with his other hand.

"I need water after that," Maria said, gazing at Jasmine and gesturing for some water. "Something to cool me down." She took off her blue cardigan. "Is it hot in here?"

I forced out a cringe-worthy laugh—a wave of pleasure filling my core—and glanced at Enji who sat at the bar by himself, staring toward us. "You know that he's a demon, right?" I said to Maria, trying my hardest to make conversation.

Eros moved his fingers faster around my clit. I could feel every single ridge of his cock pressed against my inner walls. He leaned close to me. "Ride me," he whispered into my ear with such dominance.

God, I shouldn't have begged him to take me here. I should've waited.

Maria looked back at Enji and placed her hand on Zane's. "I know."

"Now," Eros whispered, growing impatient.

I moved my hips slowly on him, listening to him groan almost inaudibly behind me. My fingers dug into the table, paling against the dark wood. I stared at Maria, trying not to give away that Eros's dick was growing inside of me, that it was pressing against my g-spot every time I cocked my hips back, that his fingers hadn't stopped massaging my clit.

"I'm actually..." She smiled wide, eyes filling with lust. "Okay with it." Zane smiled down at her, to which she responded with, "For now."

After a few moments of complete silence, Zane turned to Eros. "Did Dani tell you about Rebel?"

DESTINY DIESS

"You went to Rebel?" Eros asked, tucking a strand of hair behind my ear. "Tell me about it."

I opened my mouth to speak, but he started to move his fingers harsher around my clit. I clenched hard on his cock, my pussy pulsing on him. "I went... and... Zane was there... and..." I gulped, my heart pounding in my ears. Lord, what did I get myself into with him? "... and it was weird..."

"We had talked about the Courting Pit," Zane said. "She doesn't know who she's going to invite into the court yet."

"She'll figure that out soon," Eros said. His fingers stopped moving around my clit, and I thought he would actually give me a chance to speak. "Isn't that right, Dani?

But as soon as I parted my lips, Eros slapped my swollen clit hard with his palm.

I jumped up in the seat, my breasts pressing against the table, my mind a hazy mess, pleasure shooting through my entire body. "Yes," I said in one shaky breath. "I'll be choosing soon."

Zane stared at me for a moment more, then glanced over at the bar. He nudged Maria and whispered something into her ear. Enji jingled a pair of keys in his hand at the bar, and Maria's eyes grew big and wide. She nodded up to him.

Damn, Maria. Going to a Lust Room for the first time.

After she raised her eyebrows suggestively at me, they slid out of the booth and turned toward the bar. I relaxed against Eros, thinking she'd leave, but then she turned back around to face me. "Oh, I forgot to ask. Did you take my Gucci purse when you left by mistake? You know, the baby blue one with the navy strap?" Maria furrowed her brows. I shook my head, and she asked, "Do you know where I might've put it? I've searched the entire damn house, even Trevon's room for it."

"Maria, that purse was a decent size. Are you sure it's not lying around somewhere?"

"I'll look again... But after the ah-may-zing dreams tonight."

78

She threw me a wink and curled her arm around Zane's, walking toward the Lust Rooms.

I gazed back at Eros. "They better not do anything to her. I don't need any more demons like Trevon."

"They're sex demons, Dani." Eros thrust hard up into me and curled his hand around my neck. "The worst they'll do to her is fuck her senseless. And... she won't mind that. At least..." He brushed his lips against my ear. "You didn't."

CHAPTER 15

"Would you rather that I fucked you in a Lust Room, on our palace balcony, or right here?" Eros asked in my ear. He had already started—I didn't want him to stop now—but with everyone around, I wanted to leave. He growled deeply in my ear. "Because all I want to do is bend you against this table and pound into your tight, little pussy until you're begging me to stop."

My core tightened, and I continued to move my hips back and forth on him, the pressure in my core rising each time. "At home," I said... but I refused to move off him.

He snaked a hand back up my throat and pulled me closer to him, smirking against my neck. "Are you lying to me, Dani?" His voice was impeccably low in my ear, his scent chaining me to him.

"No." Lie.

He chuckled, the sound making his chest rumble and my pussy tightened even more. "Haven't I always told you that you're a terrible liar?" he asked, fingers rubbing my clit again. I grasped the table and stared down at the dark wood, the candle flickering in my peripheral vision. Pleasure rose in my core.

DEMONIC DESIRES

Someone walked up to our table and slid into the booth in front of us. "Just the couple I was looking for." My body shivered at the voice.

Lucifer smirked over at us, and I glanced up. God, we just couldn't be left alone tonight, could we? I raised a brow at him, staring into those icy eyes that seemed to melt as soon as they flickered down to my breasts pushed against the table. "What do you want, Lucifer?" I asked through clenched teeth, trying to keep myself sane.

"Oh…" He chuckled, sat back, and swirled his drink. "Don't let me stop you from fucking your woman, Eros. Carry on."

I swallowed hard, placed two feet on the ground, and tried to stand. "Actually, we were just leaving to go back to Lus—"

Eros stood behind me, shoving me against the table, and grasping my hips hard. "No, we're not," he said, starting to pound into me. My eyes widened slightly, my hard nipples brushing against the upper cup of my bra. Lucifer stared between me and Eros, watching Eros's biceps flex as he gripped my waist harder and harder.

"Eros," I breathed out. "W-we should g-go."

He pushed me down onto the table, hand slipping around my waist to rub my clit. My toes curled, and I grasped onto the wood to keep myself steady.

"So," Lucifer said, watching me. "I was thinking about the Courting Pit and—"

"Lucifer…" I said through clenched teeth. I was in the middle of a sex bar getting pounded into by Eros, and Lucifer thought it'd be a good time to chat. "Can't this wait?"

Eros curled his arm under my right leg and tugged it into the air, giving him better access. He spit on his fingers and smacked them hard against my swollen clit, rubbing it harsher than he had before. My leg trembled in his hand, my claws digging into the wood.

81

DESTINY DIESS

"I'll take that as an invitation to be part of your court," Lucifer said, sipping on his Vemon. "I also wanted to talk about—"

"Sure." I gazed over at him, watching the candle flicker off his eyes. "Whatever you want."

"Whatever I want?" His lips curled into a smile, his apple scent coming off of him in waves. He gazed up at Eros. "You hear that, Eros." Eros tensed behind me, as if he knew something that I didn't. "Whatever I want."

Lucifer leaned forward in his seat, forearms on the table, hand grasping my chin. "And if I want you?"

My eyes widened, my pussy clenching. Me? Lucifer wanted me? Out of all the people in the entire world, Lucifer wanted a taken woman. I shouldn't have expected anything less from him. Eros had offered to spend another night with him. I just had to say the word...

But I hadn't asked for another night with anyone yet. I was trying to hold myself off, trying to teach myself that this was enough, that I didn't need someone else to feed off of—even if it was just sexual energy.

Eros groaned in my ear, his fingers moving faster. "Cum for me, Dani."

Lucifer slid it hand down to my throat and tightened his grip. I parted my lips, my teary eyes staring right into his icy ones. I let out a moan, my entire body trembling as wave after wave of pleasure rolled through me. Eros stilled inside of me and pulled out, his cock coated in my juices. He zippered up his pants.

A thousand thoughts were buzzing through my mind, but the most prominent one was... that maybe this would be how the Courting Pit would go. I'd be in a room with a bunch of demons who watched me fuck.

It might not be as bad as I thought it'd be... right?

"This is what the Courting Pit will be like, isn't it?" I whispered, wanting confirmation. I pulled down my dress and gazed around at all the demons who were throwing glances my way.

82

DEMONIC DESIRES

"Someone will challenge me..." Like Kasey or another envious demon. "... and I'll have to fuck everyone to show them I deserve the crown."

"Yes," Eros said.

I took a deep breath. All I hoped was that I didn't lose control in the pit and start sucking people's souls for no reason at all.

Lucifer crossed his arms. "Are you expecting someone to challenge her?" he asked Eros. "You know that's the only way to end up in the Pit."

Eros tensed and glanced from me to Lucifer to the candle, his eyes darkening a shade. Without him muttering a single word, I knew that he thought someone would challenge me. Nobody knew who I was. Sathanus was spreading lies about me. And the Envies wanted the throne. It was bound to happen.

Lucifer raised a brow. "You don't believe in Dani?"

"I believe in Dani. The kingdom is just in chaos right now, like it always is after someone murders a commander."

Lucifer turned his attention toward me. "If you don't want to attend the Courting Pit, you don't have to, Dani. All you have to do is prove yourself beforehand, so nobody challenges you." He lowered his voice and leaned forward. "They have no reason to question you right now. They don't know who your mother is. All they know is that your father was Asmodeus and that you killed a heir with a single kiss." His lips curled into a smile. "Now, all you have to do is to make them fear you."

83

CHAPTER 16

I hopped into Trevon's car and into a tsunami of his cologne. My mind buzzed with dark, sinful thoughts. And though Javier hadn't bothered me since yesterday at The Lounge, I couldn't stop thinking about what Lucifer said. The words, "make them fear you," shouldn't have made me feel so... so... powerful.

It was so wrong, but I couldn't stop thinking about how I made Javier fear me, when I crawled on top of him and took everything that ever mattered right from him in one sinful, steamy moment.

Trevon stared at me from the driver's side, his solid grey tie a bit off centered. I pressed my lips into a smile and silently choked on that man's cologne. God, why was he wearing such a putrid scent today? His natural valerian scent was fine enough—it almost smelt heavenly, not that I knew what Heaven smelt like. But this... I scrunched my nose... was terrible.

"You ready?" Trevon asked, showing me his pearly whites.

After nodding my head, I stared straight through the windshield and smiled. Today would be a good day. We would visit the nursing home like we always used to, see all the old smiling faces,

DEMONIC DESIRES

hopefully see Mr. Saunders—one of the older men who loved Trevon.

Fifteen minutes later, Trevon held the door open to Harmony Grove Nursing Home for me. I walked into the quiet lobby, my heels clacking harshly against the tile. A nurse greeted us at the front desk, asking us to put on name tags and gesturing toward the front spacious rooms.

Some residents were watching TV on a dated flat screen. Others were sitting in their wheelchairs and staring out into the garden outside. Trevon placed his hand on my upper back and guided me into the room. "God, I forgot how nice these people have it."

"Nice?" I asked, arching a brow and sticking my name tag onto my sweater dress. This place was... decent, if you had to live in a nursing home. It definitely wasn't the best in the city though.

"They got a flat screen in every room, games, people who wait on them." He glanced around the room, placing his hands on his hips and sighing in admiration.

"I don't think that's how it works, Trevon..." I said. Besides, he had a TV at the apartment. I helped him move it a few days ago. And... he had so many games at his bar: pool, darts, even foosball. Why was he jealous of some cheap board games?

I grabbed his wrist and tugged him toward two patients who had just started a puzzle of a tabby cat. The women gazed up at us, and I knelt next to one. "Can we help you ladies?"

The one with short, curly gray hair smiled at me, her shaky fingers picking up a piece. I pulled up a chair and sat next to Trevon, creating two small piles of the end pieces and the middle pieces.

We finished the puzzle with the help of a couple older gentlemen that were a bit too excited to join us in two hours flat. One of the men wiggled his eyebrows at me, and I stifled my uncomfortable laugh with a smile. A nurse wheeled him away, leaving Trevon and me by ourselves.

85

DESTINY DIESS

"He had the hots for you," Trevon said, chuckling tensely. There was something in his voice that I couldn't quite place. He glanced down at me and almost immediately widened his eyes. "Dani..." He paused for a moment. "Dani, your eyes."

"My eyes?" I asked, furrowing my brows. "What about them?"

"They're glowing."

I stiffened. Shit. Shit. Shit. Shit. Shit. My demon was on edge. She had to be... But why was she coming out now? I didn't feel the faintest bit lustful. I didn't have any sinful thoughts running through my mind.

Trevon paused, gaze flickering between them. He brushed a strand of hair out of my face, and I slapped his hand away from me. Now was not the time. I had to go into the bathroom.

"They're beautiful, Dani." He didn't take his eyes off of me. "White."

"White?" I repeated. "They're glowing white?" Before he answered, I hurried toward the bathroom, locked the door, and stared into the mirror. The whites of my eyes were glowing, a white film growing over my irises and pupils.

Angel.... I... my angel.

I couldn't speak. My breaths were coming out in short rasps. I stared at my reflection, not having seen such innocence since I was younger, since Mom had been around, staring at me with her eyes glowing white.

My lips quivered, then eventually curled into a smile. "Damn," I said, eyes twinkling. My demon abilities festered so quickly that I thought it would take me over completely. I never thought I'd see myself as an angel.

Trevon knocked on the door. "Dani, are you okay?" he asked. After staring at myself in disbelief for another five minutes, I opened the door and walked out, a huge smile on my face.

Nothing could ruin this day.

Nothing could ruin the fact that I had an angel buried deep inside of me.

86

I hadn't lost her... not yet.

"Trevon," I whispered, curling my arms around his waist, overcome with so much emotion that I couldn't hold myself back from pulling him into the tightest hug I had ever given anyone. "Trevon, I have an angel. She's real."

"She's beautiful, Dani."

"Look who it is!" someone shouted. Mr. Saunders strolled down the hall toward us with his walker, the green softballs on the bottom almost as bright as an Envy's eyes. "My favorite couple is back."

I pulled myself away from Trevon and smiled. "It's nice to see you, Mr. Saunders."

When he reached us, he stopped. "I thought for a second you two had broken up. I heard Dani came by herself last time."

"Actually, we—" I started.

Trevon curled his arms around my shoulders and tugged me into his chest. "Still going strong." Trevon held out a hand for Saunders to shake, then Trevon grabbed *my* hand and brought it to his lips like Eros had done the first time I met him. What the— Trevon smiled down at me, lowering his voice. "Smile, Dani. It's Saunders."

I forced a smile on my face, despite the immense discomfort that I felt at that moment, because Mr. Saunders had been here for at least ten years and didn't have much time left. After he chatted with Trevon for a few long minutes, I waved him off. "Well, it was nice seeing you again." I dug my nails into Trevon's forearm. "We'll be back soon."

"Okay, kiddos. Next time I see you... better be some babies on the way."

My eyes widened, and I tugged Trevon out of the nursing home and into the snow. As soon as the front doors shut, I slapped him hard on the arm. "What the hell was that?"

He stared at me, brow raised, and walked to his car. "What was what?"

I stopped in the middle of the parking lot. "Why did you kiss me and lie to Saunders like that?"

He shrugged his shoulders. "Why does it matter? He's an old man. We were his favorite couple—a damn good couple. I wasn't going to ruin the last few days he had left." He opened the driver's side door and hopped in the car. "Besides, wouldn't you rather be known for being with someone like me instead of... Eros?"

My brows furrowed. What had gotten into him so suddenly? Where was this coming from? I hurried into the car, brushing off the snow on my boots before slamming the car door. "What are you talking about? Why are you so jealous?"

"I'm not jealous," he said, backing out of the parking spot, his voice dripping with envy.

"Yes, you are."

"Fine." He slammed on the breaks. "I am." His brown eyes were blazing with an emotion that I hadn't seen before. "But that's because Eros doesn't deserve you. I do."

"You do?" I asked. "The man who cheated on me with Javier deserves me?"

"You know that I was under his influence."

"Well, I was under Eros's influence but I didn't sleep with him. Hell, I didn't even kiss him."

"Don't you see, Dani? They ruined our lives and our relationship. If it wasn't for them, we'd still be together. We'd still be us."

I stared at him in absolute confusion. Why was he acting this way? First, he's jealous of the people in the nursing home. Next he made a sly comment about the older man being into me. Now he wanted me again?

"We would've broken up anyway, Trevon," I whispered, staring out of the windshield. The words had left my mouth, but I didn't know if I believed them. If Eros hadn't corrupted my mind, I probably would still be with Trevon because I loved him. But now I loved him as a friend. We could never be anything more than just friends, even if it was demons who had driven us apart.

CHAPTER 17

*A*fter Trevon parked his car in the garage under his bar, I gave him an awkward goodbye smile—still reeling from earlier—and hurried down the sidewalk toward the exit. "You're not gonna to stay for a drink?" Trevon shouted after me.

I turned around and shook my head. "I have to go see Eros."

"Just one, Dani." Trevon leaned against his car, voice tense. "It won't hurt."

"I have to go," I said, staring from Trevon to the exit of the garage and watching the snow drift down from the white sky. "I'll see you soon. Thanks for coming with me." And, with that, I zippered my coat and walked into the slush.

What the hell had gotten into him? Was he trying to get me drunk so I'd admit my deepest, darkest desires to him? If he was... boy he had another thing coming. All my desires were filled with lust-filled nights at the Lounge and a cute waitress in a little black dress and Lucifer with that sinister smirk and *wrath*.

Javier flashed into the back of my mind, and I took a deep breath. His maroon eyes were burned into my memory, haunting me every chance they got. I thought my angel would stop them, but here they were again.

DESTINY DIESS

I gazed down at my feet, frowning at my wet and soggy boots. Maybe if I pestered her enough, Dr. U would give me some meds. I'd do anything to stop this before it got worse. And if Dr. U couldn't help me, maybe someone in Hell could. Lucifer's kingdom had healers, talented healers.

Someone stood in the middle of the sidewalk, blocking my way. I glanced up, my eyes widening for a moment. Standing with her hands on her hips and dressed in the ugliest navy rip-off Ralph Lauren jacket, Samantha glared at me. Her green eyes narrowed in pure envy.

"What do you want, Samantha?"

She clenched her jaw and stepped toward me. "Stop hanging out with Trevon. He's mine."

"Well... he doesn't act like he's yours." I clenched my hands into fists. "He asked me to get a drink with him earlier," I said, watching her get even angrier. "Even told me he wanted to get back together."

A growl clawed its way out of her throat. She stepped toward me again, poking a finger into my chest. "You touch him again, and I'll make your life a living hell."

I raised a brow at her, trying to suppress my smirk. If Samantha only knew that I lived in Hell... and that it wasn't that bad there. With the Garden of Passion, Fervor Crisps for days, Eros, and—

Her fingers curled around my jacket, and she pulled me closer. "Don't you smile. Stay the fuck away from him."

I clenched my jaw and pushed her away. "You don't order me around, Samantha. I do as I please." Rage bubbled in my stomach at her audacity. "Don't you—for a second—even think about fucking with his head either. Trevon deserves so much more than you." I stepped closer to her. "If you fuck with him, I promise you to make *your* life hell."

All she did was fuck with people. She wouldn't change. She'd drag Trevon down, hurt him more, make him hate himself.

90

"We need to stop her," Javier said. *"Kill her. Slaughter her. Drink her blood."*

She dug her nails into my wrists and broke my skin. My gaze refocused on her, my eyes even widening. My hands were around her throat, and I was squeezing tighter than I had squeezed Javier's neck. Samantha's cheeks flushed, her eyes watery. I let go of her and backed up slowly.

Damn it. Damn it. Damn it.

I could hear Javier's chuckle in the back of my mind, and I tensed.

Samantha huffed. "Fucking wrathful bitch," she said under her breath. Then she stormed away from me, her brown hair bouncing on her shoulders and her baby blue knock-off purse hanging off her forearm.

"Oh, my god," I said under my breath. My hands trembled as I texted Dr. U a swift: *Meet me at Ollie's tomorrow morning. I need your help.* Then I shoved my phone back into my pocket and headed straight for the portal.

God, whatever was happening to me was far stronger than I thought it was. How did I lose control? How was Javier taking over my body? I swallowed hard... If Dr. U couldn't do anything for me, I would have to go to Eros about this.

My mind was buzzing with a hundred different thoughts when I turned down the alleyway toward the entrance to The Lounge. I slammed right into someone's back and glared up at whoever it was. "Watch it," I seethed, feeling so much rage.

The Wrath that I had bumped into in Chastion turned toward me, his eyes flashing red. Jagged teeth, a rugged exterior, a scar running down the side of his face, he growled, wrapped his hand around my throat, and shoved me against the side of the building.

Every moment that passed, he tightened his grasp. But all I could think about was that I had let these hallucinations get bad. Really bad. I blamed this asshole for *me* bumping into *him.*

"You really don't know who I am, do you?" he asked, staring

down at me. Each word was thick with venom, and the fire in his eyes reminded me of the flames from Wrath that licked my toes in my dream. The lava. The decay. The ash.

A growl clawed its way out of my throat, and I shoved him away. No, I didn't know who this man was and at the damn moment I didn't care. I pressed my lips together and walked deeper into the alley where the goons always hung out. When they saw me, they nodded their heads and started creating a portal from Earth to Hell.

"Such a shame." He stormed after me, snatching one of my wrists in one hand and the other with his barbed tail. "You don't recognize an old friend." He grabbed my chin in his free hand, brushing his thumb harshly against my lower lip. "I could've done so much to you, if I wanted."

My heart pounded against my chest. I didn't know what he was saying. Hell, I didn't understand it. All I wanted was to sink into my bed sheets with Eros when I got home, try to forget about everything that happened today, and see Dr. U tomorrow.

I didn't know if I was sad about Trevon, angry at Samantha, or fucking scared that I was turning into a monster who couldn't control her innate urges to suck someone's soul.

So, again, I slammed my hands into his chest and pushed him away. The black mystical portal drifted in a circle against the side of the building. I stormed over to it, listening to him follow me.

God was testing me today. I get threatened by someone who wanted Trevon—my ex-boyfriend and her ex-boss—all to herself and then run into another damn lunatic.

"You're wrathful. The Queen of Lust is wrathful." The Wrath shook his head. "It's festering. What's the kingdom going to say, knowing that this pretty little mind of yours is corrupt? That you're unstable?"

"What is your damn problem?" I asked, turning on my heel and watching him step into the portal. "Are you another one of the demons who doesn't believe in me either?" I clenched my jaw and stepped toward him, wrapping my hand around his throat. "Well, let me tell you, *Wrath*... I will be the queen. I will follow in my father's footsteps. And if you get in my way, I'll take your soul, cut off your horns, and keep them as a fucking trophy like I did with the heir to Sathanus's throne."

CHAPTER 18

The next day, I shook the snow off my coat and walked into Ollie's Diner. Whistling kettles, the scent of pure coffee beans, and the light pink staff uniforms, Ollie's was buzzing with people this morning.

Dr. U sat in a red booth near the windows, staring out at the slush on the sidewalks. After quickly gazing around for any sign of Mycah, I slid into the booth opposite of Dr. U. She smiled widely at me and sipped on her black coffee mug. "So…" She arched a hard brow. "What's wrong?"

A waitress that I hadn't met before placed a mug of Jazz Mint tea in front of me and took my order. When she disappeared behind the bar, I glanced back at Dr. U. "Why do you think something's wrong?"

"Don't give me that," she said, brown eyes staring pointedly at me. "I can see it in your eyes."

I took a deep breath. I had never asked Dr. U to prescribe me any drugs before because I knew that it was stepping over a fine line. But I needed something to stop these hallucinations before they got worse. I wanted to control them before the Courting Pit. I couldn't go into the

Crowning Ceremony worried about Javier saying something to me.

"Fine," I said, rubbing my sweaty palms on my jeans. "Something's wrong."

"What is it?" she asked.

It was so difficult to admit that Javier was torturing me aloud. But I had to tell someone, and that someone couldn't be Eros. Not yet. I wanted him to know because it'd be the right thing to do... but I couldn't tell him I'd been dreaming about his brother. That would break him. It would break us. It could hurt everything we had built together.

"The dreams of Eros's brother haven't stopped..." My brows furrowed together. "They're just getting worse. I'm even starting to hallucinate." I took a deep breath and lowered my voice. "I feel like he's taking over my life, but he's a dead man..." I gazed out the window, watching the snow collide with the window and melt almost immediately.

Dr. U grasped my hands. "It seems like his death is weighing on your consciousness."

Of course, it was. I *killed* him. Trevon probably still had nightmares about killing someone with his bare hands... but Trevon and I were different. Trevon was possessed by a demon. I *was* a demon who was struggling to control my urges.

"Dr. U... I need medicine." My words came out so quietly that I barely heard myself. "I need these hallucinations to stop. It's getting hard to control them."

Her eyes widened. "No," she said. "Absolutely not."

"Please," I said.

"You know I can't do that." She furrowed her brows at me and brushed her fingers against my knuckles. "Dani... why is his death bothering you this much?"

I sucked in a deep breath, not wanting to relive that moment. Just thinking about taking his soul, about feeling the pleasure pass through my lips... it made me crave *more*. I swallowed hard.

DESTINY DIESS

"I have to tell you something..." I said, needing to get it off my chest.

Dr. U had become a mother-figure to me and... I wanted her and Mom to be proud. But how could she be proud of her daughter who had killed someone with a kiss, had been dreaming of having sex with that man, and couldn't stop the urges she had to kill someone again?

"What is it, Dani?" Her voice was soft, and I closed my eyes, picturing Mom.

When I reopened my eyes, I tried to open my mouth, tried to tell her I killed someone but nothing would come out. She would be disappointed in me. What if she judged me for it? How would she even react?

Ollie's door's bell jingled, and my gaze shifted to the front of the cafe. Kasey and Mycah walked in and stood near the cashier, waiting for pickup. My eyes widened, and I hopped out of my seat. I needed to talk to Kasey too, even more.

After muttering a quick "hold on" to Dr. U, I hurried toward my friends. "Kasey!"

Dressed in a cute white halter top and black jeans, Kasey turned away from me when I approached. Mycah gave me a small, sympathetic smile, her chubby cheeks rounding. She interlocked her and Kasey's fingers in support.

"Kasey," I said. "Please talk to me." But she didn't turn around. Instead, she stood with her back turned toward me. "Kasey, please." I grasped her wrist lightly, and she pulled her hand out of my grip.

"Look, Dani," Kasey said, lips set in a tight line. "I don't want to talk to you right now. My parents are dead because of you. My brother is dead because of you. And Eros won't even listen to me *because of you.*"

Her words hurt because every single one of them was true. Most of her family was dead because Eros wanted to protect *me.* Though I couldn't feel her pain, I understood it. My parents were

96

dead because of hers. It hurt to lose Mom... but to learn that I had lost Dad too... it killed me. I didn't want her to hurt.

"You're hurting." I reached for her hand. "I know how it feels."

She ripped herself out of my grip and shook her head. "No, you don't. You don't know what it's like to walk in to see your mother and father dead, lying on the ground in the middle of the throne room." She narrowed her eyes at me, a vicious, grueling expression crossing her face.

Some people glanced over, including Dr. U. My heart tightened in my chest, memories of Mom lying dead in the street, of the blood gushing out of her body, of her once bright eyes lifeless. I pressed my lips together, my eyes filling with tears. "I watched my mother die because of your parents, Kasey. They killed her for power." My voice was shaky, yet it rose with every word.

Dr. U hurried over to us and grasped my arms. "Dani," she said, her soothing voice not able to calm me like it did when I was four. "Dani, calm down."

"Don't talk to me about hurt," I seethed, my chin quivering. "I've been dealing with this for my entire life."

Kasey furrowed her brows at me, her green eyes intensifying. "My parents didn't do a single thing to you."

As soon as the words left her mouth, the darkness festered inside of me. My demon begged me to release it so I could take her soul too. Her lips looked too tasty to pass up, and my wrath was too overwhelming to control.

Dr. U wrapped her arms around my torso, pulling me out of Ollie's without even getting our belongings. "They destroyed my entire world, Kasey. My entire fucking world." The door closed, and I watched her face contort into pure anger through the cloudy glass.

Snow drifted down around us, hitting my bare arms... but all I felt was an immense heat. How dare she tell me that her parents

DESTINY DIESS

did nothing to me. How dare she tell me that I couldn't understand her pain when the same thing had happened to me.

My blood was boiling. I was seconds away from losing it all and transforming into a demon right here in the middle of Fifth Ave. Dr. U grabbed my hand and hurried down the sidewalk. I gazed out into the street, imagining Mom's dead body, those piercing red eyes, the sanguine blood through my tears.

I tried to pull my hand away from Dr. U—wanting to go back to Ollie's and give Kasey more than just a piece of my mind. I wanted her to live through that day with me. I wanted her to hurt because of it. I wanted to hurt her.

Dr. U paused, took one long look at me, and shook her head. "Shit," she muttered under her breath. It was the first time I had ever heard her swear.

Before I could pull my hands away from her, she pulled me into the nearest alleyway and tugged us behind a garbage bin that stunk of rotten eggs and sewage. I ripped myself out of her grip and dug my claws into the green bin, breaking right through the metal. Kasey had the goddamn fucking nerve.

Dr. U grasped my face, her fingers brushing against my cheekbones. I could feel every single vein in my body pulsing, my vision turning dark, the hunger in my soul raging. Horns burst out of my forehead, darkness completely filling my vision.

Something smelled good, and that something was Kasey.

"Dani... Dani... calm down." Dr. U still stood in front of me, brushing her thumbs against my cheeks. I had expected her to cower in complete fear, but she stared deeply into my eyes and refused to look away. "She's hurting right now," she said.

"I've been hurting for the past twenty years." My body trembled with pure rage. "I've had a hundred, thousand nightmares of those beady red eyes."

"I know, Dani..." Her eyes softened. "But you know that you can't compare your pain with hers. Everyone hurts, and everyone hurts differently. That's the first thing I taught you, isn't it?"

98

An image of me choking Kasey with my bare hands flashed through my mind. Javier. Damn, Javier was fucking with my mind again. When I tried to look away, Dr. U forced me to stare at her. "Dani… Dani… please look at me."

I grasped her wrists, my claws dangerously close to the veins in her arms, yet she still didn't back away. She stared up at me with so much strength that it scared me. And, then, she asked, "Do you want me to tell you a bedtime story? One that your mother used to tell you?"

My body relaxed at the mere mention of Mom. A story? Dr. U brushed her palm against my hair, smoothing it out, and a tear rolled down my cheek. "A story?" I asked quietly. "A good story, one of Mom and Dad, together and happy." All I wanted was to hear their story, to know that at some point they had been happy together and that this pain resulted from something good that they shared. My eyes filled with more tears, and I wrapped my arms around her, grasping for her warmth. "Please, Dr. U."

"Sorcerer of Temptation, so fierce and passionate, seal me to your horns, to your fingers, to you everlasting lust." She grasped my face in her hands. "You used to mumble in your sleep when you were younger." She glided her thumb against my cheekbone and sighed. "Don't lose yourself, Dani. I know you're going through a lot. But don't lose the angel inside of you, hold on to her for as long as you can."

I furrowed my brows at the mention of my *angel.* "You… you knew about me?"

"All these years," she said into my ear. "There was always something special about you."

CHAPTER 19

After my chat with Kasey, I decided that I needed to talk to someone in Hell about my problems. Dr. U could bring me back down to Earth when I lost control, but she didn't understand my demons—metaphorically and literally. So, I walked into the Kingdom of Lust through the portal to meet my only friend.

Maeve stood at the portal's exit, immediately curling her arm around mine. "Tell me all the deets," she said. She pulled me onto the white stone walkways toward the Garden of Passion. "Oh!" She paused for a second, rummaged through her purse, and pulled out a brown bag. "I saved one for you."

I opened the bag and smiled down at it, my heart warming. The sweet scent of Fervor Crisps drifted through my nose. I plucked one out of the bag and sunk my fangs into it, moaning in delight. "Thank you so much."

If nobody else could help me, Fervor Crisps could.

After I had finished it, she stuffed the bag back into her purse, looped her arm around mine again, and walked with me into the garden. The roses twinkled under the pink suns, their perfume scent wrapping around every inch of my body.

When we walked through the entrance, some Lusts glanced over at us and whispered. I straightened my back, feeling a bit self-conscious. I could hear all their harsh words running through my head. *I wasn't fit to rule. Nobody would follow me. Sathanus would have my horns in less than a week of me claiming the throne.* And I wanted to snap at them, but I didn't want to lose control again like I had earlier.

Maeve rolled her eyes. "Ignore them," she said to me. "They're immature and don't know the true power you possess." Her fingers curled into my forearm. "So, why'd you want to meet? Who is fucking with you?"

"Kasey," I said. Rage pumped through my veins, and I clenched my fists. Control, Dani. "She hates me, absolutely hates me. I don't even know what I did."

Well, that was just a white little lie. I knew she was annoyed at me because I aided Eros in killing his parents. But it was well deserved and so was Javier's death. I didn't regret killing him.

"She doesn't hate you," Maeve said, picking a rose and lifting it to her nose. "She's envious. She wants the throne, just like her mother wanted the throne." She bumped my hip with hers and smiled. "What makes you think she wouldn't try to take it from you? Envies will do anything to get what they want." She winked at me, her green eyes glowing ever so softly. "I would know."

I exhaled through my nose. If Kasey was anything like her mother, she would try to kill me for the throne. She'd kill her own brother and one of her best friends. Unless, after all this time, Kasey was just pretending to be friends with me.

"I just thought she was different." I lowered my voice, hoping that I didn't sound naïve by letting my human emotions blur reality. "I thought we were friends."

Maeve stayed quiet and gazed down at her feet, a guilty expression crossing her face. "Demons aren't always who you think we are. We hurt people. Sometimes we do it unintention-ally, sometimes we do it intentionally, and sometimes we can't

DESTINY DIESS

control ourselves." She curled her red-painted toes into her sandals. "That's one of the hardest lessons you'll learn down here."

I pulled my hand to my chest and drew my thumb across my ring. For twenty-four years I had grown up with best friends who had never betrayed me. Then when I met Eros, everything spiraled out of control. First, Trevon. Now, Kasey.

Dad was right. There would be friends that I could love from afar but couldn't trust. I just hated that Kasey would be the one I couldn't trust. We had so many memories together.

Tears welled up in my eyes. "My father..." I started, my voice raspy.

Don't cry, Dani. Kasey isn't worth your tears.

But she was. Kasey, the one person I had grown closest to, was worth all the tears I had. I didn't want to lead this kingdom without her. Why couldn't she see that her parents had hurt me and Eros? Why couldn't she see how bad they really were?

"She's a traitor." Javier's voice echoed in the back of my mind, fury laced around every one of his words. "Just like Eros when he killed his parents. All I wanted was to make you a fucking Lust Queen. All I wanted was to give you a taste, but you took my soul."

I pressed my lips together and pushed away my tears. This thing was driving me crazy. My entire world was falling apart. But I had Eros, I had Lucifer, and now I had Maeve.

Maeve stopped in the field of flowers. "Your father, what?" She furrowed her brows.

"My father told me I couldn't trust some of my closest friends. I should've listened."

"I thought you never got a chance to meet him."

"I didn't. He..." I thought back to my journal he left me and smiled. I wanted to go look through it some more. Maybe he left a note about Mom in there, hidden away. "He left me his journal."

"His journal?" she said, lips curling into a smile, eyes sparkling green. She threw her arms around me and pulled me into a tight

DEMONIC DESIRES

hug. "If you have his journal, you have everything you need to rule the kingdom, right?" When I nodded, she tugged me toward the castle. "Well, then, forget about Kasey. You don't need her. You don't need anybody to help you rule."

I paused, then smiled. She gazed back at me, her dark hair blowing in the light wind. God, I had barely known her for a week, yet she had so much confidence in me. Her hands dropped to mine, eyes following when her fingers brushed against my family ring.

She tugged her hand away, as if it burned her like Mom's pendant had burned Eros the first morning I met him. "Did your father leave you this ring too?" she asked, staring down at it. The color turned to black from her fingers, then slowly faded back to pink.

"Yeah," I said, smiling down at the heart-shaped pendant.

"It's really beautiful," she whispered, eyes playful. "I wish I had one."

CHAPTER 20

When I reached the castle, I walked to Dad's office, sat in his big comfy chair, and opened his journal. His tattered letter to me fell out of it, and I grasped it in my trembling hand. Maeve had comforted me about Kasey, but Kasey was the least of my problems.

Javier was still fucking with my damn head.

Between hiding my angel from all of Hell to holding my demon back on Earth, I felt like I was holding all of Heaven and Hell on my shoulders. I smoothed out the letter on the oak desk. The words I didn't want to read seemed to come right off of the page.

There are people who want our blood and our souls.

I have seen the strongest men and women sucked into the darkness, never to return.

Demons are not afraid to betray.

Maybe I was one of those women who was being sucked into the darkness. Maybe Kasey was one of those who would betray me to gain power. And maybe Sathanus's threats were more than just empty threats, maybe they were promises.

DEMONIC DESIRES

I took a deep, shaky breath. How did I let it get this bad? Could I really rule an entire kingdom? I felt like such a fraud, walking down the streets, trying to get people to believe in me when I didn't even believe in myself.

Tears fell onto my paper, and I leaned back in my chair and clutched my ring, curling my arms around my body. I gazed down at the paper, then at the journal, re-reading the damn prophecy about the Unholy Trinity. On top of everything, I had to worry about the three strongest demons in Hell rising up and starting a war with the Heavens.

Shit was too much. I needed a damn release. *Another soul.* Not another soul. *Someone to devour, someone like Eros.* No, not Eros.

After closing my eyes and shaking my head, I heard the office door open. I expected to see Eros walk in and save me. But when I opened my eyes, I saw my worst nightmare walk through the door with a smirk on his lips and wrath blazing in his maroon eyes.

Javier.

My eyes widened at him, and I shook my head, unable to believe that he was real. He closed the door behind him and sauntered into the room, his taut chest bare, a mere sheet hanging off his hips.

Big, thick horns. Swollen muscles. Lips that would've melted me, if I didn't know better. I stood, listening to my chair roll and hit the wall behind me, and dug my claws straight through the pages of Dad's journal. What the hell was this?

"What's wrong, Dani?" he asked, stepping toward me. He smelt like peppermint, that alluring scent of peppermint that I had inhaled the day I killed him. And when I looked into his eyes, I felt that same surge of power. It rushed into me, consumed me, became me.

"Is it too much for you?" He drew his finger against my desk and walked all the way around it until he stood directly in front of

105

me. His lips parted, fingers so close to mine. *"All you have to do is surrender all your power to me and we can rule all the kingdoms in Hell."*

I swallowed hard. "No." I pressed my hands to my ears. "You're not real. You're not fucking real." I shook my head from side to side, my brown hair whipping into my face.

He stepped even closer to me and snaked his hand around my throat. Though his touch was gentle, there was something overwhelmingly evil about it. It struck fear right into my bones.

"Get away from me! Get away from me now!" I screamed at the top of my lungs and stumbled back into the wall.

"Dani... Dani!" someone said. The voice sounded distant, yet so close, like it was just out of reach.

Javier took another step toward me. Damn him. Damn him. Damn him. I curled my hand around his throat, squeezing and pushing him away. "I said to stay away from me!" I shouted, staring at the man who had tried to fuck me. From my core to my breasts to my lips, I felt the lust and wrath clawing its way up my body, desperate to consume his lonely soul yet again.

My hunger reawakened.

He collapsed to his knees, and I collapsed with him, wrapping my other hand around his neck. When he closed his eyes, I could feel him gasp for breath. He lifted his fingers and brushed them against my forehead.

My mind suddenly cleared, and I saw nothing but... Eros.

Eros knelt in front of me, his cheeks a light pink. My hands were wrapped tightly around his throat. I gulped and loosened my grip slightly, but I didn't know what was real anymore. This could be another one of my visions. Javier could just be fucking with me again.

"Dani," Eros whispered. "It's me."

"Prove it," I whispered back, tears welling in my eyes. "Prove to me it's you."

Eros closed his eyes, and a wave of pleasure surged through

DEMONIC DESIRES

my body. All of his memories rushed through my mind. Him holding me outside of Ollie's in the pouring rain after I had puked, me staring up at me as he wiped off all my makeup after the Halloween party, the smile on my lips when I had taken my first bite into a Fervor Crips. They were memories that Javier could never have.

I took a deep breath, tears streaming down my cheeks, and dropped my hand. Eros... it was only just Eros. "Eros," I breathed, watching him catch his breath. "I-I'm so sorry. I didn't mean for that to happen."

He sat me on Dad's chair and crouched between my legs. "What's going on?" he asked me, pushing away my tears with his thumb. "What have you been keeping from me?" From the look in his eyes, I could tell that he had known something had been going on for a while now.

I didn't want to tell him. I didn't want him to hurt.

I hugged my arms around my body, my chin quivering. "I'm having visions and hallucinations of... of..."

"Of what, Dani?" His voice was so tender, and I hated breaking his heart.

"Of Javier," I whispered.

Eros's calm demeanor changed into a tense and shielded one in less than a second. "Of Javier?" He reiterated his name in disbelief and in pain. His fingers dropped from my face.

I grasped his hands, desperate to feel him. "I'm sorry," I whispered. "He's taking control of me and... and I can't do anything about it. I'm sorry for not telling you sooner. I just... didn't want to hurt you."

Eros paused for a few moments, his eyes flickering back and forth. Then he picked me off the chair and walked with me out of the room. "Come on, Dani."

"Where are we going?" I asked, tucking my head into his chest.

"Lucifer's kingdom."

107

DESTINY DIESS

"Lucifer's kingdom? Are you... are you taking me to The Chains?" I asked, because I didn't want to go to The Chains. Not after what I had seen happen to Trevon. I didn't want that pain on top of the hurt I already had.

"No, I'm taking you to one of Lucifer's healers."

CHAPTER 21

Just outside Lucifer's Castle, there was a small building made almost entirely out of ice. Eros led me inside. My gaze traveled from the azure walls, watching the light permeate through the edges, to the grand white chandelier in the center.

Demons from all kingdoms waited on booths of ice. Eros pulled me under a large parabolic arch to a man with small ice horns. "Do you have an appointment?"

"She needs to see a healer as soon as possible," Eros said, nodding toward me. It was the first time I heard him speak since we had left Lust. On our way here, all he had done was grasp my hand tightly, and it was making me nervous. Maybe this was worse than I originally thought, or maybe I just made Eros more angry that I thought I would've because I didn't tell him sooner.

"We don't have any open appointments today, Lord Eros."

"She'll see him next," Eros said without room for argument. He took my hand and pulled me to a booth. When we sat, some demons looked over at us and whispered amongst themselves. My demon wanted to break free and kill each one of them for

DESTINY DIESS

talking poorly about me yet again. But, instead, I gazed down at my legs.

God, Dani, control yourself. Not here and definitely not now.

I took one glance up at them, my claws lengthening and cutting right through my palms. If I had the chance, I would dig my claws right into their necks and kill them a—

Eros growled, and they quieted down. He placed a hand on my thigh, fingers digging into my exposed skin. He still didn't say anything to me, just sat there with a clenched jaw.

He was mad. Scratch that, he was furious that I hadn't told him about Javier sooner. But... could he blame me? I didn't want him to believe all those nasty things his parents had told him about not being a true incubus because I was sleeping in his bed yet dreaming of another man.

"There you are," Lucifer said, sauntering into the room. "Didn't think you two would actually be here." He cocked his head to the side, a slight smirk on his face. "This place is for the lowly peasants, if you ask me." He sat in the booth across from us, wrapping his hands around the back of the seat and kicked one leg over the other. "So, what has Dani here today?"

The vein in my neck pulsed with rage, Javier sensing the tension. "I'm here to see an actual doctor. Not you, Luci." My words came out harsher than I expected, and suddenly my entire body felt like flames. I could feel the blaze of Wrath, the fire under my skin, crawling it's way through each layer of muscle, making me burn even in the coldest kingdom in Hell.

I sat there and stared at the blue wall, trying not to see red. But the color blurred my vision, my fangs ached for blood, my soul needed more, needed another soul to bind with, to consume, to devour.

"What's gotten into your woman's panties?" Lucifer asked, arching a brow at Eros. "Certainly not you, if she's acting like this."

Eros's fingers dug lightly into my inner thigh. "Javier," Eros

110

DEMONIC DESIRES

said. Though his voice was low, Javier's name rolled off his tongue with so much distaste, like even when he was dead Javier was still hurting him.

Lucifer's grey eyes turned a shade lighter and widened. He sat up and chuckled. "Oh, Dani, now we're talking." With his lips curled into a smile, he said, "The heir to Wrath. You've got yourself into some trouble."

Before I could respond, a pretty young woman with chocolate brown hair and small icicle horns peered from a doorway. "Commander Asmodeus? Dr. Xiexie will see you now."

I glanced briefly at Eros who still didn't say anything, then I patted his thigh. "Don't wait for me. I might be awhile. I'll find you back at the castle." Then, without sparing Lucifer another glance—because I knew that if I did, my demon would snap—I followed the nurse into another room.

Though I expected the patient room to have a granite cauldron, a plethora of healing potions, and glass crystals hanging from the ceiling, the room looked like one back at Lust. With a grand bed, done up with the finest red-silk blankets, and small candles burning in the corners, the room had an almost sensual feel to it.

"Commander," someone said from behind me, placing their hand on my shoulder. I jumped up in surprise and turned around to see a man towering over me. Blue eyes, chillingly cold fingers, horns about a finger-length long, he stared down at me. "Sit."

I sat uncomfortably on the bed. My feet didn't touch the floor, so I kicked them back and forth and twirled my ring on my finger. I gazed around the room some more, hoping to find something to keep my mind sane. If I snapped here and lost control and—I furrowed my brows at the doctor who had started removing his pants. "Why're you taking off your clothes?"

"You're here to relax, aren't you?" He paused for a moment. "Lucifer—"

"Probably told you I needed to be fucked, didn't he?"

DESTINY DIESS

I drew my tongue against my fangs. Taking this man's soul would be so easy. He was almost inviting me to do it. And his neck... his neck looked oh-so-inviting for me to just plunge my teeth into, to suck his soul right out of his bloodstream, to lie there in a puddle of his blood and drink him dry.

But I wouldn't do that because I had control.

"Put your damn clothes back on," I said, clenching my jaw.

He smoothed out his pants and stood across from me with his head bowed. "My apologies, Commander."

"Don't apologize. I just need help."

"What can I help you with?"

I paused for a long moment and swallowed hard. Would admitting this to him make me look weak in the eyes of yet another demon in Hell? Would this secret break me? What if word got out to everyone around that I was this crazy half-angel, having hallucinations of demons?

"Everything we say here is confidential?" I asked, making sure that while the room looked nothing like Dr. U's, the rules were the same and that nobody would find out about this secret that I've been hiding for so long.

He parted his lips, as if he was thinking about it. "If—"

"No ifs, unless you want me to tell Eros about what you thought this little meeting was really for." I raised a sharp brow. "Or I could just take care of you myself."

He bowed his head again. "Information here is private, Commander."

"Good," I said. "Because if it's not, I'll be back to finish you off."

And, then, I laid back on the bed with my hands over my face and told him about all these disturbing visions that I kept having of Javier, how they weren't going away, and how he was slowly taking over my mind.

Dr. Xiexie paused for a moment, brows drawn together. "This is a common symptom of soul taking. The consumer will feel

112

DEMONIC DESIRES

some of the same intense emotions for a few days after they take the soul because that victim's soul binds to yours."

My brows furrowed. "Are you saying that once I kill someone, I will never be free of them? I have to carry around their souls for the entirety of my life?" And why the hell didn't Eros tell me this?

"Usually demons become desensitized to it, and it rarely takes such a heavy toll on someone for more than three days." He paused for a moment. "I've seen it common among humans... but half-human and half-demons rarely have this strong of effect for this length of time."

I pressed my lips together and lowered my voice. "I'm not half-human. I'm half-angel."

His eyes widened, and a chilling gust of wind hit my exposed flesh. "You're Fatima's daughter, aren't you?" He hurried over to the window and closed the blinds, peeked his head out the door to look for bystanders and then locked it. "You can't tell anyone that you're half-angel. Nobody. Do you hear me."

"I haven't told anyone besides Eros and Lucifer."

"Those who supported the previous leaders in Lust will hunt you down and kill you. They hated that Asmodeus was with an angel. They slaughtered the poor man for it and hung his horns as a warning in the center of Chastion."

They hung Dad's horns in Chastion? Were his horns still there? Could I get them back, so I could have a piece of him too?

I took a deep breath and pushed those thoughts to the back of my mind for now. "I don't plan on telling anyone." I swallowed hard. "But would this have an effect?"

"Yes, this changes things. This changes many things." He paced back and forth, tapping his foot. "I know very little about angels, but I have vast knowledge about demons. I can tell, based on what I do know, that Javier's mind—if he is strong enough— could control you. He feeds off both lust and violence." Xiexie gazed right at me. "You can't help feeding off of lust yourself, so —whatever you do—don't feed into his violent side."

113

DESTINY DIESS

"Do you have a potion or something that could fix me?"

"There's nothing I could do for soul-taking. Demons usually know what they're getting themselves into when they take a soul. The best I could recommend is to surround yourself with friends and... I don't say this often... but go out and do something good."

"Should I repent?"

Though his expression was serious, his lips curled into a smirk. "You don't repent in Hell, especially not for Javier. These hallucinations started after you killed him, correct?" he asked. I nodded. "Then, you must follow these instructions... hold on to your lust, it is what will keep you alive down here. But don't let go of your goodness, because it will keep you sane."

CHAPTER 22

When I walked out of Dr. Xiexie's *office*, I took a deep breath. Though I still didn't have this entire thing under control, it was a relief to understand what was happening to me, to figure out a *cure*, and to tell someone else about my angelic side.

After pulling myself together, I passed the demons in the waiting room who were still giving me that side-eye and found my way to Lucifer's castle. The two blue suns blazed against the white horizon. I squinted my eyes and stared up at the tall castle and even taller glaciers surrounding it.

The guards opened the palace doors for me, and I wandered into the grand foyer. The interior was a unique cross between white granite and cold, dark stone. Soft voice echoed through the empty castle, and I followed them up the stairs until I reached the top floor.

Apples and cinnamon drifted through the air. I brushed my fingers against the walls and walked toward the voices, inhaling the alluring mixture.

"This is a good thing," Lucifer said from the room at the end of the hallway.

There was a long pause. "How is it a good thing?" Eros asked, his voice tense.

"This is what Dani needs." Lucifer paused, and I leaned against the wall next to the open door and listened. "Isn't it, Dani?"

Damn it.

I peeked into the room to see Eros and Lucifer sitting on one of the large leather couches, Eros's arm was draped against the back of the seat, his body turned toward Lucifer. His arms, painted with dark tattoos, were flexed. Lucifer whirled a drink of Vemon in his hand and smirked at me. They were closer than I had ever seen them.

When Eros met my gaze, he pulled his arm away and turned toward me. I walked into the room and sat next to him, placing my hand on his thigh. "What do I need, Lucifer?"

"Javier." Lucifer placed his drink down on the glass table. "This will give you just the edge you need to make everyone fear you."

"This is not what I need to make them fear me." I arched a brow at him. "I can do that all by myself." Not that I actually wanted to make anyone fear me... I already feared this power.

"You can't suppress it," Lucifer said, the words coming out as if he knew that they were true. He walked around the couch until he stood directly behind me, placed his hands on my shoulders, and squeezed lightly. "You want more souls," he said into my ear. "It felt good to take Javier's, didn't it?"

"Lucifer, don't," Eros said, staring back and forth between us, his eyes slowly growing black. There was a tenseness in his eyes and in his demeanor that I had never seen. Something about it made me uneasy, as if he was *worried* about me.

I tensed and swallowed hard, my heart pounding against my chest. Lucifer's cold lips brushed against my ear. "But you're afraid of the power you hold because you don't know how to control it. You think about drinking people dry, stealing their

DEMONIC DESIRES

soul, letting it bind to yours. Once you start, you don't know if you'll be able to stop."

"Lucifer," I said, my voice wavering. My insides tightened, and I tried hard to control myself. But it seemed like all the doctor's advice went right out of the damn window because when the Devil talked into my ear, I listened. Not because it was good advice, but because deep down it was exactly what I wanted to hear.

"Let it control you."

My visions blurred with red and black streaks. I dug my claws into Eros's thigh, my fangs aching. I closed my eyes and inhaled the aromatic scent of apples and only apples.

"Lucifer," Eros warned.

"Surrender yourself to all those devilish thoughts."

Something inside of me snapped, and I turned around, snatching his jaw in my hand. It felt so fragile, like I could break it within seconds. Lucifer's wicked icy eyes gazed into mine. "Somebody's growing a backbone."

I growled and gazed down at Lucifer's soft lips. Apples. His scent grew stronger by the second. I inhaled deeply, and Eros grasped my hand tightly to hold me back from taking everything from Lucifer. My head snapped in Eros's direction, and I snatched his chin in my other hand, my lips parting in pure delight.

Two souls to feed me.

"Do it, Dani," Lucifer whispered in my ear. "Kiss him. Take his soul."

My eyes flickered to Eros's lips, the lips I had kissed so many times. I tugged him closer to me and pressed my lips to his, succumbing to all my sinister thoughts. His lips tasted like cinnamon; His mouth tasted like cinnamon; His breath tasted like cinnamon... but I craved apples. Delicious apples.

"Why don't you share all that pent-up tension?" Lucifer said to me.

117

DESTINY DIESS

I pulled Lucifer closer and pressed my lips to his. Something about him tasted different than Javier. I felt that power, that energy transferring between our lips. My hand curled around his throat, and I tugged him even closer.

He tasted like Heaven and Hell, like the good and the bad, like pure sin.

My demon took control. I shoved him down onto the couch next to me and crawled on top of him. Lust ran through my veins. An insatiable urge for power built in my core. I wanted as much as I could get. I squeezed his throat tighter, yet no matter how hard I squeezed, nothing happened.

No soul. No death. No divine feeling rushing through my veins.

Lucifer pulled away, eyes playful. "What's wrong, Dani? Can't take my soul?" he asked. I stared down at him, brows furrowed in confusion. Why hadn't it happened? "Your little magic doesn't work on me."

Eros growled. "That's not how it works, Lucifer, and you know that." He grabbed my wrist to pull me away, but Lucifer placed his hands on my hips and stared up at me with those sinister blue eyes.

"How does it work then, Eros?" Lucifer's fingers slipped under my shirt and moved in small circles against my bare hips. I swallowed hard, my hunger for power being replaced with a need for lust. He curled his fingers into my skin. "You can control it, Dani." He smirked. "When you really want to."

CHAPTER 23

"She has nothing to worry about, Eros," Lucifer said, wrapping his arms around my waist and sitting up. The scent of apples drifted into my nose, making my head feel hazy again. And though I didn't fully trust his words, I found comfort in them because I couldn't take Lucifer's soul and because his cold thumbs were rubbing small, rhythmic circles around my hips.

His eyes were like pools of ice, layer after layer of blue. He tilted his head to the side, his full lips curling into a smirk and strands of his platinum hair falling into his face. Lust pumped through my body, and I broke our gaze and glanced at Eros.

I could smell his arousal from watching me straddle one of his greatest friends. And I relaxed further on Lucifer's lap, feeling his hardness underneath me, and reached for Eros's hand. "Come."

Eros clenched his jaw, gaze drifting from me to Lucifer who pulled me even closer until my breasts pressed against his chest. "You do want to prepare your woman for the Courting Pit, don't you?" Lucifer asked, pressing his hips against my core.

Though I didn't need to spend another night with Lucifer, I

DESTINY DIESS

had been craving it. Something about him being inside of me, about Eros watching us, about me being filled with passion made me ache for more.

I grinded my hips into Lucifer's, letting Eros watch, and then pulled Eros onto the black leather couch with us. Eros settled next to Lucifer, his black eyes on me. I placed my hand on his black jeans, squeezing his thigh lightly, claws digging into the thick material.

He brushed his fingers against my chin, making me look at him. Tingles erupted on my skin, my heart racing in my chest. "Well," Eros said, lips brushing against mine. "I'm waiting."

He didn't have to tell me what he was waiting for in order for me to know. I grinded my hips harsher against Lucifer, my core tightening. His cock was hard against the front of his pants, pressing against me. All I could remember was the last time he was inside of me, pounding me against the bed, and Eros watching from the corner.

My hand traveled to the front of Eros's pants, and I wrapped my fingers around his bulge, grasping his cock and rubbing it back and forth at the same pace I moved my hips on Lucifer.

Groaning softly, he relaxed against the back of the couch for the first time tonight. Cinnamon drifted through the air, mixing with the fresh scent of apples. Eros placed his hand on mine and moved it with me. With every moment, he was growing harder and bigger. "Touch me," I whispered, my core aching. "Please."

Lucifer snuck his hands under my shirt and slowly peeled it off my body, leaving me in a lacy black bra. His chilling fingers brushed over the thin lace, making my nipples hard. Eros grasped my chin softly. "Take off your clothes for us, Dani," he said.

My pussy clenched, breath catching in the back of my throat. I crawled off Lucifer and stepped out of my pants, standing in my panties. Both of the men relaxed against the couch and stared at me.

DEMONIC DESIRES

"Everything," Eros said, eyes lingering on my hips. I gulped and reached behind me, undoing my bra, letting my straps fall down my shoulders, and throwing it off of me. My breasts fell out of it, bouncing slightly. Lucifer smirked at me and placed a hand against the front of his pants. Goosebumps rose on my skin, my nipples hardening even more at the frozen air. I crossed my arms over my chest to keep warm.

"Drop your arms," Lucifer said.

"But it's cold."

"And?" he asked, eyebrow cock. "I want to see your tits."

I clenched, dropped my arms, and glanced at Eros who looked at me and then my underwear. "I said, 'everything,' Dani. Let's see how wet you are for us."

After taking a deep breath, I pulled down my underwear and kicked them to the side with my foot, standing completely naked in front of two damn-sexy demons. "Are you wet?" Eros asked. When I nodded, he smirked. "Show me..." He cocked a finger in my direction. "Come."

I crawled onto the sofa next to him, and he pulled me over his knee, rubbing his hand against my ass. I placed my palms on Lucifer's thigh and gave Lucifer a hot open-mouthed kiss on his lips.

Eros smacked my ass hard, making my skin tingle. I let out a soft moan, my pussy clenching. He did it again, and my breasts bounced against Lucifer's chest. Lucifer fondled one of them, tugging lightly on my nipple. Eros slapped me again, and I rested my forehead against Lucifer's, letting out another moan.

Eros grabbed my horn and pulled me back. "Get his cock wet before you ride it," he said into my ear. Lucifer undid his pants and pulled out his hard cock. My eyes widened slightly, but I arched my back and dipped my head, swirling my tongue around the head of his cock.

When I started to slowly take him into my mouth, Eros trailed

DESTINY DIESS

his fingers lower and lower down my ass until he was playing with my folds. "So wet, Dani," he mumbled, sliding his finger into me. He pushed my head further on Lucifer's cock until he hit the back of my throat. My cheeks flushed, not even having all of him inside of me yet.

I gagged and took more of him into my mouth, my eyes watering. "Deeper, Dani," Eros said. Pressure built in my core, the feel of Eros's fingers moving skillfully inside of me, curling at just the right angel and at just the right time.

My lips met the base of Lucifer's hips, and I tried to breathe through my nose. Eros pumped his fingers into me, and I clenched harder. When I needed to breathe, I pulled away and Eros pulled his fingers out of me, rubbing my ass again. "Good girl," he said, releasing my horn.

Lucifer kicked off his pants and pulled me on top of him, his fingers digging into my waist. I sat on his cock, his head pressing against my entrance. Eros watched as I placed my hands on Lucifer's chest and slowly lowered myself onto him. The pressure grew in my core.

My claws dug into Lucifer's chest, and I moved my hips back and forth on his cock, the pain being quickly replaced with pleasure. Lucifer spit on two of his fingers, reaching behind me to gently rub them against my ass, preparing me for Eros.

I moaned softly and arched my back even harder. Eros leaned closer to us and rubbed his fingers against my clit. "Does that feel good?"

I furrowed my brows and clenched hard on Lucifer, heat warming my core. "Fuck her harder," Eros said to Lucifer. They both sat back and watched me as Lucifer pumped faster into me, hitting my cervix and making me clench. "Faster," Eros said.

Lucifer gazed over at him, eyes on his lips. "Faster?"

Eros stared back at him, black eyes hazier than I had seen them in a long time. The tension between him and Lucifer was almost unbearable but so very hot. Eros's fingers continued to rub small circles around my clit, driving me higher and higher.

Their lips were inches apart from each other. Eros glanced over at me with struggle in his eyes. All I wanted was for them to press their lips to each other, to kiss while they both touched me.

"Do it," I whispered, staring between them, my brows furrowing together. Eros turned back to Lucifer, his nose grazing against his. "Please, it'll make me cum," I said, trying to hold out.

And when Eros pressed his lips to Lucifer's lips, I bucked my hips back and forth, letting out a loud moan. Wave after wave after wave of pleasure rolled through my body as they kissed. Their tongues wrapping together, their soft lips on each other's. My legs trembled as I continued to ride out my orgasm.

I stared at them, like Eros had stared at me and Lucifer weeks ago. Something about the way they touched each other, about the way their lips moved in sync made me feel like they've done this before together. It felt so natural and so utterly passionate.

Eros pulled away, wrapped his hand around the back of my head, and placed his lips onto mine, kissing me hard. Then he stood up and walked behind me, taking off his clothes. I listened to his pants unzip and felt him press into my backside.

He grasped one of my horns, pulling me to the side, and placed his lips on my neck, sucking on the skin. When I let out a throaty moan, he pushed himself inside of me, so both of them were filling me up. I threw my arms around Lucifer's shoulders, pressing my breasts into his chest and letting them both fuck me as they wanted.

Letting them have me was... liberating. I didn't understand why. I didn't understand how, but a feeling of vigor washed over me when I was with them, a feeling that made me feel powerful and alive.

Lucifer grabbed my ass, spread it apart for Eros, and buried his face into my hair. I tugged on the ends of his and moaned, letting Eros thrust into me hard from behind. After a few more

DESTINY DIESS

hard thrusts, Lucifer bucked his hips hard into me and came inside of me.

After hearing Lucifer groan, Eros grabbed my horn, pulled me back, and pressed his lips to mine. I kissed him back hard—riding out one of the best damn orgasms of my life. And that simple feeling of passion and fervor, of desire and sin, could and would destroy me one day.

CHAPTER 24

The next day, Eros and I locked ourselves away in our palace to prepare for the Courting Pit and the Crowning Ceremony. With everything happening lately, it was difficult to keep track of the days. But there was less than a week left, and I was beyond nervous.

I walked from our bedroom to downstairs, tightening my red silk robe around my waist. The scent of Fervor Crisps and milk drifted through the castle, and I followed it, thinking I'd find Eros in the kitchen.

So many thoughts had plagued my mind last night, the biggest one being that Javier was still lurking inside of me, but hopefully he'd be gone after today because I would be spending time with the people I cared about.

After pushing open the kitchen door, my eyes widened. "Commander," Jasmine said, giving me a small smile and gesturing toward a seat at the table. "Good morning." Instead of her typical tight black dress she wore at The Lounge, she was wearing a fitted blush-colored dress with a swooping neckline, sleeves that hung off her shoulder, and ruffles near the knees.

All my worries seemed to disappear when she turned my way,

DESTINY DIESS

her breasts pressed tightly against her dress. I swallowed hard and tried to push away my sinful thoughts. Eyes on the table, Dani. Eyes on the damn table.

I sat, a blush crawling onto my cheeks, and kicked my legs back and forth. Her skin was a mocha-color, cute little freckles on her nose. She wasn't just sexy. Jasmine was beautiful. A true demon of Lust.

She placed a strawberry strudel in front of me. "For you," she said, gazing at me, her eyes a hazy brown. I watched the strawberry cream ooze out of the crisp dough and pressed my thighs together. Calm, Dani, calm.

"What are you doing here?" I asked, carefully breaking off a piece with my fork.

Cinnamon floated through the room, followed by quick footsteps. "You wanted her here, didn't you?" Eros curled his hand around my throat from behind, making me look up at him, and placed a kiss on my lips. When he pulled away, he smirked down at me, his dark brow arched. "Hmm?"

"Yes," I said, cheeks flushing even more. "I did."

"Good morning, Lord Eros," Jasmine said, bowing her head.

Eros nodded his head and sat across from me. "Good morning, Jasmine." He grabbed a plate of Fervor Crisps from Jasmine and bit into one. "You'll be free on Thursday night for the party before the Crowning, correct?"

Jasmine nodded her head. "Yes," she said, glancing at me. "I'm free for whatever you or Commander Dani would like me to do."

I swallowed my food and thought about letting her do more than just cook for us.

Eros eyed me from across the table, then looked back at her. "We need one more bartender," he said. "Unless... Dani has other plans for you that night."

"No." The word came out quicker than I wanted it, making me sound suspicious. My cheeks flushed, and I stared down at the plate. Every time she was near me, every time I smelt her sweet scent of chocolate, every time she smiled at me—even if it was just a flirty smirk from across the bar—it made me excited, flustered, and even embarrassed. Though Lust demons mixed with each other all the time, I had grown up in a different culture where *liking* someone else while in a relationship was a HUGE no, nevermind flirting with someone else.

Thankfully, Eros leaned across the table and plopped a crisp into my mouth. "Lucifer wants to meet at The Lounge today, so I'll be there for most of the day. You're welcome to come."

I shook my head, trying to think clearly. "God, Lucifer likes you."

Eros glanced down, staying quiet for a few moments. "I'm the only one who can tolerate his pride for more than a few hours. Of course, he likes me," he said with a smirk.

But there was more. Ever since that kiss the other night... I couldn't stop thinking about it. Something about them together like that made me curious about what exactly they were to each other.

Part of me wanted to pry, but the other part of me couldn't stop glancing over at Jasmine who had turned away and was very sensually watching the extra strawberry cream drip off a spoon and into a brown glass bowl.

Eros smiled at me and stood. "Well, if you're not coming, I'll be off."

My eyes widened. "Um... maybe you should stay a bit longer... I, um..." I glanced at Jasmine, my core clenching. She brought the spoon to her lips—her eyes on me—and licked off the cream.

Instead of saving me, like I wish he had, Eros chuckled. "I'm sure you'll enjoy Jasmine's company just fine." Then he walked right out the door.

Jasmine watched me from the other side of the kitchen, still playing with the bowl of cream and her spoon. I glanced over at her, a wave of heat warming every inch of my body. She smiled

DESTINY DIESS

and stepped toward me, trailing her finger against the counter. "Do I make you nervous, Commander?"

God, this woman said six damn words, and I was a goner already. If anyone knew how to flirt, it was her. More than the Triad. More than Lucifer. Hell, almost more than Eros... but nobody could surpass him.

"I didn't say you did," I said, sitting back and trying hard not to break, afraid that if I let myself get too excited, Javier would take control. But my entire damn body betrayed me when I stood up, grabbed my plate, and walked over to her.

"Have you had breakfast?" I asked, breaking off a piece of strudel with my fork. She stepped closer and brushed her fingers against my forearm. My nipples hardened against my silk robe, and she glanced down at them and smirked.

You're in control, Dani. Act like it.

I placed the plate on the counter next to her and pushed the fork to her lips. "Eat," I said. She wrapped her full lips around the fork and sucked off the strawberry cream. "Do you like it?"

Her eyes clouded with haziness, and she stepped closer to me, breasts brushing against my arm. "I rather be eating something else."

"Yeah?" I asked, my voice barely a whisper. All I wanted her to do was push me against the counter, slip her hand under my robe, and do things to me I had only let Eros do. "Why don't you?"

She stepped between my legs and pushed me against the counter. "Is that what you want?" she mumbled against my ear, sliding her leg between mine, making my robe fall open to the side. Her eyes were a hazy black mess, and strands of her hair were falling into her face. "Because I'll do anything to please my commander."

I grasped her chin, forcing her to look at me, and inhaled her scent. "That's—"

"Dani!" someone called from deep within the palace. My gaze

128

flickered from Jasmine to the door, never having heard the female voice before here. Jasmine's fingers slipped under my robe and brushed against my underwear, making me clench.

Maeve appeared at the door, mouth ajar. I released Jasmine's chin and stepped away from her, trying to push away all the dirty, little fantasies running through my head. Maeve's lips twitched into a smile, the happiness not reaching her emerald eyes. "Sorry to interrupt, but I thought we were going to Rebel today."

Jasmine brushed her fingers against my forearm. "You know where to find me, if you really mean what you said." She walked out of the room, her hips swaying from side to side in her tight blush dress.

After I excused myself from the kitchen, I hurried upstairs to change quickly into some tight jeans and a swooping, red halter top. I grabbed my phone from my nightstand and gazed down at the messages from Dr. U. *"I'm volunteering tonight at the ice skating rink. Care to join?"*

My lips curled into a wide smile, and, before I left the room, I grabbed my coat because it was bound to be cold on Earth.

Maeve was walking around in the throne room when I returned, her fingers brushing against the velvet throne itself. "Are you ready?" I asked, folding my coat over my forearm.

She turned and held a hand to her chest as if I startled her. "Oh, yeah." She smiled when she saw me and continued to look around the room. "It's really beautiful in here. I've never been in a throne room before."

"Well," I said, curling my arm around hers. "It's good that I'm inviting you into my court in a couple days, then, isn't it?"

While most of Lust would watch the Courting Pit and the Crowning Ceremony, I had to invite a few special people to be by my side in the throne room to bear witness to my crowning. And because Kasey was out of the picture, I wanted Maeve because she had been one of my constants down here.

"Really?!" she asked.

DESTINY DIESS

"Yes." I smiled and pulled her toward the exit of the castle. "I don't know or trust many people here, except you and a few others in the palace."

She broke into a fit of contagious giggles, giddy about what I had told her, and walked with me through Chastion. We stopped briefly for Fervor Crisps at Annen's Bakery and found our way into Rebel, the day *and* nightclub in the center of the city.

Even in the morning, Rebel thrived with people either dancing, getting drunk off Passions, or flirting hard. The light toward the back of the club was a soft pink today, and though there were about twenty free booths, Maeve pulled me toward the back, as if she knew exactly where she was going.

And she did, because the Triad was sprawled out on a couch, all looking oddly satisfied this morning. "So, this is why you wanted to come here," I said, arching a brow at them. Zane had his back turned toward me, his shoulders slumped forward, less uptight than he usually was on Earth.

When Axel noticed us, he held out two full glasses of Passion on the table. "I knew you wouldn't be able to resist coming to see me, Maeve," he said, burying his face in her neck when she sat down next to him.

Her cheeks flushed, and she playfully pushed him away. I sat down next to her, watching him and her fall into an easy and very flirtatious conversation. Zane and Enji sat across from them, rolling their eyes. I arched a brow. "I'm hoping Maria is still in one piece."

Zane chuckled and said, "Maria is fine." Then he gazed at me from across the table. "You don't have to worry about a thing."

CHAPTER 25

"So," I said, awkwardly walking next to Zane toward the ice skating rink after our get-together at Rebel. Maria had asked him on a date, but Zane didn't date. He fucked, apparently. Him and Maria had spent more time with each other, but I didn't like the fact that he was part of the Triad because I didn't want the same thing that happened to her with Javier to happen again. "What's going on between you and Maria?"

He brushed some snow off his shoulders and pulled his jacket tighter around his torso. "We're just friends."

"Just friends?" I asked, crossing my arms over my chest and trying to keep myself warm. God, even Lucifer's kingdom wasn't this cold... or maybe I had just been getting used to it down there. "You seem like you're more."

We passed the road where *it* happened—Mom's murder, and I glanced down it, seeing those piercing red eyes in the middle of the street, staring back at me. I could feel Javier's fingers in my throat, could feel him clawing his way back into my head.

My jaw twitched, a weirdly innate urge to snap coursing through my veins, but I took a deep breath and stepped closer to Zane until my arm began brushing against his with every step.

DESTINY DIESS

Familiarity. Close friends. Goodness. I repeated it in my head like a hymn, hoping that Javier would disappear. Zane paused for a moment and gazed at me, the same haziness I saw earlier in his eyes. Instead of scurrying away like I should have, I arched a brow at him and said, "Well?"

"We're just friends, Dani," Zane said, turning back. "We fuck sometimes, but that's it."

"But you like her," I said, teeth chattering slightly.

"I like many people."

The crosswalk light flashed white, and we crossed the street to the outdoor skating rink. "Well, don't break her heart because I won't let Maria get hurt again."

For the first time in a long time, he chuckled, deep and throaty, a laugh that got me all hot and bothered. "And what will you do to me?" he asked. There was a light flirtiness in his voice.

While I didn't love flirting with just anyone, it was the typical way of speaking to another Lust demon. And, if I wanted to be queen and to get people to like *and* trust me, I'd have to pick up their mannerisms.

"You'd like to know, wouldn't you?" I asked, lips curling into a smirk.

He smiled again, turning his hazy eyes away from me and inhaling deeply. "You're more tempting than you think you are, Dani."

I glanced up at him and walked into the square. The rink was filled with about a hundred people, bright lights shined down upon the ice. It was almost seven o'clock on a weekday and this place was poppin' tonight.

Maria sat on a black metal bench, staring at her phone screen and trying to put on some mascara. Zane excused himself and found his way to her, and her eyes almost immediately brightened. I frowned, wondering if she had caught feelings too fast for him.

After shaking off the thought, I walked to a small building

132

where there were lockers, a place to buy food, and a smiling Dr. U who stood behind the counter, handing out shoes to couples and children.

I kicked the snow off my shoes before I entered, then took off my coat, hanging it on a coat rack in the back. The heat was on full blast, blowing directly into my face as I stood next to Dr. U. "What do you need help with?" I asked.

"Are you good with money?" she asked, nudging me to the concession stand. I arched a brow at her and walked over. And for the next three hours I handed out hot chocolate and fries and the occasional hot dog.

When I had taken everyone's orders, I rested my elbows on the counter and stared out at the ice skating rink. Though it was still late and the skaters were slowly starting to leave, there was a mother and daughter skating together on the ice. The little girl with blonde pigtails was holding her mother's hand as they spun in small circles. She had the biggest smile on her face, and my heart warmed, remembering when Mom used to take me here.

We'd come here almost every week during the winter and split a basket of fries and a hot chocolate. I wished I could spend one more day here with Mom, just one moment was all I wanted. One moment to see her smile or to hear her laugh or to feel her fingers against mine.

A teenage boy walked into the room, leaving four of his friends outside in the cold. "Slurpee, please."

"We don't have slurpees," I said, brows furrowed together. It was almost freezing outside, and this kid wanted a slurpee? "We have hot chocolate."

He adjusted a baseball cap on his head. "You got a candy cane you can put in the hot chocolate?"

"Um, yeah."

"Give me three."

"Three hot chocolates?"

"Three candy canes in one hot chocolate."

I stared at the boy in confusion and poured him his drink, hooking three large candy canes into the cup which would melt down to their fragile core within the next five minutes. "Three candy canes in one hot chocolate, just for you," I said, placing the cup on the counter and watching Trevon walk through the door.

The kid took the cup and walked outside, gulping it down like it wasn't even burning his tongue. Trevon stared at the kid and turned back to me, jaw clenched. "Just for him, huh?"

I waved my hand in the air. "It's nothing."

He leaned over the counter in front of me, getting a little too close, and smiled, glancing back at the boys one more time. "Remember when we talked about having kids?"

My eyes widened, and I furrowed my brows at him. What the hell? I leaned closer to him, so none of the other volunteers could hear the fight I was about to get in with him. "Trevon, we talked about that one time. Years ago." I shook my head. "We're over."

Trevon shook his head and glanced away. "Because Eros broke us up."

I rolled my eyes. I couldn't believe he wanted to have this conversation here and again.

After tugging on my coat, I grabbed his wrist and pulled him out of the building, so nobody could hear us. "Because you cheated on me," I said, whisper-yelling and poking him hard in the chest.

Why were we running in circles, fighting about the same senseless things over again?

"I was under Javier's influence."

"Well, I was under Eros's influence and I didn't sleep with him. Hell, I didn't even kiss him while we were together."

"You're the fucking Queen of Lust," he said, as if it were an excuse.

I crossed my arms over my chest and grabbed his arm, forcing him to look at me. "Which is why I should've jumped on Eros the moment I saw him, but I resisted. I didn't physically touch another man like that because I wanted to make us work." I crossed my arms over my chest, watching the snow melt against his dark skin. "And you didn't seem to have a problem with us being broken up until recently. So what is your damn issue?"

After he paused for a long moment, he shook his head and walked away from me. I stared at him from across the rink, lips curled into a frown. What had happened to him? One minute he was fine that I was with Eros, the next he was jealous of him. Never, and I mean never, had he brought up Eros in conversation beforehand. Not when we broke up. Not when he turned into a demon. Not when I announced to him that I would be queen.

"Dani," Dr. U called from behind me. I glanced back to see her peering behind the door. "We'll be closing soon."

I nodded my head and turned back around for a quick moment. Trevon walked around a couple tables, where that teenager and his friends were taking off their ice skates. That man was going to drive me insane.

The sweet scent of cinnamon filled my nostrils, and I glanced behind me at Eros. Wearing a scarf and a thick wool coat that went down to his mid-thigh, he curled his arms around me and rested his chin on my shoulder. "How's it going?" he asked, placing a kiss on my neck.

For a moment, I thought I'd feel Javier's lips on me, but all I felt and smelt was Eros, which meant that this... this... *cure* might be working. At least, it was working a bit. I hadn't had another hallucination of him again.

"What are you doing here?" I asked, brushing my fingers against the slight stubble on his chin. "I thought you were heading to The Lounge with Luci?"

"He had some business to take care of," he said softly in my ear. His cheeks were a light pink, his green eyes were so comforting. "So, since I was in the city, I thought I'd come see you."

My eyes fluttered closed for a mere moment as I enjoyed him. Something about today, about right now, felt so utterly peaceful.

DESTINY DIESS

"I can finally introduce you to Dr. U!" I said, grabbing his hand and pulling him toward the door. When we walked into the room, Dr. U was behind the counter, organizing the ice skates by size. "Dr. U," I said. "This is my partner, Eros."

She glanced toward us, her eyes widening. "Eros," she said, smiling softly. "It's nice to see you again."

My brows furrowed, and I curled my fingers into Eros's bicep. "Again?"

"We've met a few times in passing," Eros said to me. "At the lounge."

I stared between the two, brow arching. He didn't fuc—

"Do you want to explain?" Eros asked her.

Dr. U blushed and rubbed her hands together. "I used to date... Eros's sister."

"Kasey?" I asked. Eros grimaced, and my eyes widened. "You dated *Kasey*, the woman we saw at Ollie's the other day?"

She gave me a tense smile. Oh, my god. Dr. U dated Kasey? My best—ex-best—friend Kasey? I could barely believe it. I glanced between Eros and Dr. U a couple times, trying hard not to think of Kasey because the last time I saw her, I wanted to rip her head off and take her soul. She'd only bring Javier back out, and I'd break just when I thought I was getting better.

"Well, I have to finish these," Dr. U said, breaking the tension between us and going back to organizing the shoes. I pulled Eros back out into the cold, letting his body keep me warm. The group of teenage boys walked in front of us, cutting us off.

"You stole my hot chocolate."

"No, I didn't."

"Why're you fucking lying?"

"Fuck, dude, I said that I didn't."

"Hey," I said to them. "No cursing."

One of the boys turned around. "What do you kno—" He stopped mid-sentence, eyes widening. Then he slapped one of his

136

friends on the chest and slowly backed up and turned around, looking... scared. "Dude, did you see her eyes?"

"She was hot."

I held a hand to my forehead, muttering an "Oh, dear lord," under my breath, and turned around toward Eros.

Though I expected him to say something snarky to me or even agree with that kid, he widened his eyes at me, his typical sinful look gone, and brushed his fingers against my cheek. "Heavens," he whispered.

"What's wrong?" I asked, brows furrowed together, scared that maybe... just maybe this wasn't working after all and I was starting to resemble Javier now. Maybe my eyes were glowing black even though I wasn't conscious of it.

"Your angel..." He smiled widely at me. "Your eyes, your skin... they're glowing." His fingers curled into my sides, and he said, "Look at me."

He grasped my face in his hands and made me look into his eyes, which changed from green to totally black so I could see my reflection. Like the other day at the nursing home, my eyes were like white stars but with black rings around the edges, and my skin was glowing just as Eros had said.

"What do you think of me?" I asked softly. Trevon had given me his opinion the other day, but I wanted to hear it from Eros. His opinion mattered more than Trevon's. Much, much more.

He stared at me for a few moments. "What do I think of you?" he asked, lips curling into one of his boyish smiles. "I love you." He took a deep breath. "Heavens, I love you so much."

There was something about that moment, about standing with Eros in the snow, about the way he looked at me, that made me so freaking warm. And I wondered if this was how Mom and Dad felt together.

Complete.

He rested his forehead against mine and brushed some hair out of my face. "You know... when I was in Heaven, I'd make

DESTINY DIESS

people fall in love with each other. That was... my *job*. A heart-shaped dagger right through the heart." He unzipped his jacket, slipped my hand under it, and ran it over his chest so I could feel the light scar under his shirt. "But this... us..."

"We're real," I whispered. Butterflies fluttered around in my stomach. While I wasn't sure what the future had in store for us, while I knew that it wouldn't be this easy all the time—especially in Hell—I placed my lips on his and breathed him in. If we could survive the Courting Pit and the Crowning Ceremony, we could survive—

"Eros," Trevon said, tensely from behind me.

I closed my eyes and clenched my jaw. One moment. One damn moment. That was all I asked for, but, of course, nothing could be that easy. I pulled away from Eros and turned around, grasping his hand and intertwining our fingers so Trevon knew not to bother me about getting back together with him.

Eros gazed at him for a moment, brows furrowing together. "Heavens, he reeks of something putrid," Eros whispered against my ear. He paused for a moment, then smacked my ass, pushing me forward. "Why don't you finish closing? Let me talk to Trevon."

After biting back a laugh—knowing Eros would say something smart to him—I walked to the building. Dr. U stood outside, dressed in her coat, talking to a petite woman. She was older with short pink hair, green eyes, and a huge smile. Dr. U glanced at me, and I wiggled my eyebrows at her flushing cheeks.

"Dr. U!" I said, approaching her once the woman disappeared down the street. "Your flirting was phenomenal!"

She playfully rolled her eyes and turned back to the rink. "That wasn't flirting, Dani. She's just an old colleague."

"A colleague that you might be going out on a date with?" I asked, gazing back at Eros and Trevon and watching Eros's lips curl into a deeper smirk as they spoke. Trevon had his arms crossed over his chest.

138

DEMONIC DESIRES

Dr. U stayed quiet for a long time, and my smile widened. "No way," I said, my heart racing. "You're going out on a date?" Not once in my entire life did I see Dr. U go out on a date. She was always either home or at the office, working. I nudged her. "Well, if you need me to help you get ready. I have the perfect team."

She laughed, her soft voice drifting through the air. "The perfect team?"

"Me and Maria will get you looking hot," I said. "Hair, make-up, nails. Anything you need."

She blushed a deeper red and smiled at me, the moonlight bouncing off her eyes. "Sure," she said. "I'd like that. I'd like that a lot."

My smile widened even more. Dr. U and I rarely spent time together anymore. Hell, we barely spent much time together at all, even when I was growing up. But... I wanted to see her so happy, just like I wanted Mom to be happy. She deserved happiness for everything she had done for me.

"How's Trevon?" Dr. U asked, eyeing the two men. While Eros was calming chatting with Trevon still, Trevon was working himself up. Breaking into a sweat. Hands clenching into fists. Fingers tugging on the ends of his hair.

After speaking some nasty words to Eros, he hurried over to me and Dr. U, eyes desperate. "Come out to dinner with me."

"No," I said, shaking my head. "I'm having dinner with Eros."

"But—"

"No."

"Dani." He reached for my hand, but I pulled it away.

"No. Why don't you go out on a date with Samantha or something? She's been bothering me about talking to you. And..." I gestured between us. "We. Are. Over."

His jaw twitched, and he walked out of the rink and down the street. Dr. U looked over at me, giving me her infamous *do-I-want-to-know?* look. I just shook my head, not wanting to even get into it right now, and told her I'd finish closing.

139

DESTINY DIESS

After Dr. U departed from the rink, Eros stalked over to me, wrapping his hands around my waist, and stuffed his nose in my hair. "Let's skate," he whispered into my ear.

"Eros, I'm closing right now. I can't." I turned around, about to walk back into the building to turn the light off, but Eros stepped in front of me with that dangerous smirk plastered on his face. "Oh, come on. You can break the rules just for me, can't you?"

My lips curled into a soft smile, and I grabbed a pair of skates for both of us. "If this is some elaborate scheme to have sex with me in public again, I don't want to do it." His eyes twinkled, and I pulled his skates away from him. "I'm being serious, Eros."

"Relax, Dani," he said, grabbing his skates from me. "It's not some elaborate scheme." He pulled on his shoes and tied them, pulling me onto the ice. "It's some scheme that I just threw together."

I narrowed my eyes at him and playfully pushed his chest. "You've been hanging out with Lucifer too much," I said. "You're picking up his mannerisms."

"Lucifer and mannerisms don't go well together," Eros said, curling his arms around me and pushing us forward.

"Exactly."

He chuckled in my ear, making me shiver in delight. His cinnamon scent drifted through my nose, and I inhaled deeply. "So, what'd you and Trevon talk about?"

"You," he said. "He wants you back, and I just let him know that if he lays a hand on you, you'd probably... maybe..." He smirked down at me. "... Take his life."

I arched a brow. "I'd take his life?"

"Or I could throw him back into The Chains." He spun me around, his hands in mine, breathing in the frigid air. "But... he smelt... weird."

"Do you think... he's possessed again?"

"I don't know. I can usually tell when someone's possessed,

the scent of a demon is overwhelmingly strong. His scent isn't *that* strong. But... it wasn't that strong last time either."

"I'll keep an eye on him, and I'll tell Zane to watch him too. I can't risk Maria getting possessed. I already lost one of my friends; I can't lose the oth—"

Suddenly, an excruciating pain split through my back, near the sides of my spine, and I grasped Eros's arm, trying to hold myself upright.

"What's wrong?" Eros asked, brows furrowed together. He grabbed my hands to steady me.

I clenched my jaw, hoping the feeling would pass, and squeezed my eyes closed. I wanted to tell him that everything was okay, that this pain was disappearing and that I'd be fine... but this wasn't the time to keep things from Eros. I learned that the hard way with Javier.

"My back," I whispered. "It hurts."

His eyes filled with darkness again, and I could see my glowing ones reflecting off of them. "Tell me where it hurts." Starting at my neck, he slowly trailed his fingers down the middle of my back, down each vertebrae until he reached the center.

I whimpered and grasped his biceps, the pain overwhelmingly strong. "It's not Javier, is it?"

"This is where it hurts, Dani?" he asked me. When I nodded my head, he gazed around and tugged off my coat. "Take this off."

"Eros," I said under my breath. "We're in public. If I get caught out here... naked..."

"Dani, listen to me and take it off," he said, his voice sounding so serious that I was actually nervous. I took off my jacket and tossed it onto the ice next to us. Another pain shot through my back. Something felt like it was poking hard against my skin from the inside.

Javier... it had to be Javier and his demon.

I swallowed hard, remembering when Trevon was in The

DESTINY DIESS

Chains and a demon climbed his way out of his throat. Javier was dead... but... but what if he really wasn't... what if...

"And your shirt," Eros said.

"My shirt?"

"If you don't take it off, it'll rip."

"Rip?"

"Dani," Eros said, jaw clenched. "Now."

I gulped and pulled the shirt over my head, leaving me in the black lacy bra I had worn only to seduce Eros in later tonight. Eros eyed my bra, his eyes oddly not turning hazy, and I arched a brow at him. "What? Do you want me to take this off t—"

My legs buckled underneath me, another pain flaring around the sides of my torso from my spine. I grasped onto his biceps, holding myself up, and he wrapped his arms around me, pushing a hand through my hair and rubbing my scalp rhythmically.

"What's going on?" I asked, my lips trembling.

"This is going to hurt," he said, trying to soothe me. "The first time always hurts."

"What the hell are you talking about? Why are you talking in circles?" I asked, digging my claws into his flesh... but my nails hadn't turned into claws. No matter how hard I tried, I couldn't break his skin with my blunt nails. So, I stared up into his dark eyes to see my eyes glowing a bright white.

"Your wings, Dani."

And, within that moment, my knees buckled for real this time, only Eros caught me and held me up by the waist. I could feel my skin stretching and tearing, and could hear the ripping of flesh. Something grew from my back, protruding at angles I didn't even know existed.

I buried my face into Eros's chest and let out a scream, hoping he would muffle it. The last thing I needed was to attract the attention of someone like a human or a demon, especially when I couldn't control this, whatever it was.

When the pain had subsided, that lingering ache never really

DEMONIC DESIRES

leaving me though, I let go of Eros and stood up, the sudden weight almost too heavy on my back. I gazed behind me, my eyes widening.

Oh, my god.

They were huge.

At least seven feet wide and standing a solid foot above my head, my wings were grand with black streaks near the base—at least that's what I could see and white feathers near the edges.

"I haven't seen angel wings in thousands of years," Eros said breathlessly, eyes wide in amazement. "The last time I saw wings this grand and filled with this many feathers... were Lucifer's before he fell." He brushed his fingers against my wings and smiled.

My wings were as grand as Lucifer's once were? Did that mean I wielded as much power as he did? Or maybe even more...

"But Lucifer's looked nothing like this," Eros continued. "They were pure white." He grasped my hands and stepped away, admiring me. "And a feather would fall each time he sinned."

I wanted to ask Eros how he knew Lucifer's feathers fell off, but I pressed my lips together.

"Yours don't look like they'll ever fall, just transform into the darkness." He trailed his fingers down my spine and near the blackened feathers. "Your father was right, Dani. You'll rule as Hell's most powerful queen."

Not Lust's most powerful queen. Hell's.

CHAPTER 26

I tugged off my peacoat, folded it over my forearm, and stepped into the chilly waiting room at Dr. Xiexie's office by myself. Eros was off preparing Lust for the ceremony, which was coming up faster than I expected; Lucifer was doing God-only-knew what with him. But after last night and experiencing my angel for the first time, I needed to come back here to talk to Dr. Xiexie about this.

Some demons lingered in the room, chatting aimlessly with each other. I sat on the sofa and played with the ends of my coat as I waited, trying to ignore the subtle stares the Lusts and Envies were giving me.

Focus on the good things, Dani, like your angel. I closed my eyes, imagining my grand wings stretching the length of this room, my eyes shining like two white orbs surrounded by a ring of darkness, my skin glimmering even in the shadows.

"The Lust Queen's horns will hang in Chastion before the Crowning," the Lust said to the Envy.

I pressed my lips together. Focus, Dani. On better things. On virtuous things. On heavenly things. Something other than fire and ash and pure destruction.

DEMONIC DESIRES

"Looks like she's already going insane," the Envy said, nudging the Lust.

I swallowed hard, anger pumping through my veins. Think of Eros, Lucifer, Dr. U, and Jasmine... But all I could think about was who was feeding them this bullshit. My entire body ached to snatch their necks and snap them after I found out.

"A human can't rule Lust." The Lust chuckled. "Even if Sathanus doesn't kill her, she won't last a single day, trying to tame Eros and the rest of us."

Something inside of me snapped, and I stormed over to him, grabbed him by the chin, and wrapped my hand around his thin, little throat. "All you should worry about is how disrespectful you're being to your new queen who will rule the Kingdom of Lust with or without your approval. If I hear another word from you, I will snap your neck and take your soul without question, so I suggest you stop questioning my authority."

The Lust's eyes widened, and I pressed my lips together, trying to stay calm because while I couldn't hear Javier's voice ringing inside my head and I couldn't see his red eyes staring right at me... I could feel him stirring up trouble, instigating my wrath, and making me angry again.

Before Javier took complete control of me, I released the man's neck and glared down at him. "Why don't you run back to Sathanus or whoever the fuck is starting all this drama and tell them that if they want to shame me, they should come to the damn ceremony and see what happens?"

The Lust bowed his head, an unusual look of terror crossing his face. "I apologize, Commander."

The Envy crossed his arms over his chest, sneering at me. "What are you going to do to us, if we don't? If you want to kill us, kill us now. Prove yourself to everyone here. Earn your respect."

Wrath pumped through every one of my veins. My fingers ached to slide around his neck and feel the life pumping out of

145

DESTINY DIESS

him. All I could see were the thousands of ways I could make him hurt and the one way I could kill him so damn easily that he wouldn't feel a single thing.

"Commander Asmodeus," the nurse said from the doorway. "Dr. Xiexie will see you now."

My heart thrashed against my chest, Wrath's fire warming every single inch of my body. It took everything inside of me to bite my tongue. I gave him one last look and stormed to the nurse.

"That's what I thought," the Envy shouted. "A human isn't capable of what you claim to have done. You'd never be queen. You'd never live up to your father's reputation. I'll enjoy rubbing off on your horns when you're dead."

I hurried into the back hallway before I snapped, my vision shifting between a clear to a grey to a black color, and I stopped mid-stride. Jaw twitching. Heart pounding. Blood boiling. I could see Wrath in my vision, the ash falling from the sky, the flames licking my toes, the heat inside of me.

"Commander," the nurse said cautiously. She stood in front of Xiexie's office, lips pressed together, eyes wide in fear. "Commander..."

For a split moment, I reached my hand out for her neck, wanting to break something... But, instead, I brushed my thumb against my ring and thought of Mom swinging me around in circles at the ice skating rink, the white ice reflecting off her eyes. And my wrath slowly dissipated.

Lord... at least I could kind of control it now.

After taking a deep breath, I walked into Dr. Xiexie's office and shut the door behind me. Unlike the last room, there wasn't a bed in this one but a grand oak desk, floor-length and foggy windows, and an enormous bookcase with titles in *Demoniac*, an ancient demon language, that I couldn't quite read yet.

Dr. Xiexie stood by the windows, staring out at Pride. "It's beautiful, isn't it?" He smiled to himself, then turned to me and

DEMONIC DESIRES

sat at his desk. "I didn't expect to see you so soon. Is everything okay?"

I sat on a white cushioned chair and placed my coat in my lap. "I... um... got my wings last night."

"Your wings?" he said quietly, eyes wide. "Angel wings, I suppose?"

I didn't know if they were solely angel wings, especially with those charcoal-colored feathers, so I said, "They're white and black." I paused. "And Eros thinks they won't shed when I sin like angel wings do."

"Black feathers?" He furrowed his brows, searched his bookshelf, and pulled out a thick leather-bound book, flipping through the pages and shaking his head. "No angel has black feathers... And there have been no accounts of feathers that don't fall off when you sin."

There was some noise in the hallway, and he lowered his voice. "When I was an angel, I found that feathers fall off fairly quickly. Lucifer's took longer, which ranked him as one of the strongest demons in Hell... but not falling off at all... It just doesn't happen."

"But I've sinned so much already." Every single night. "Don't you think that I just wouldn't get wings at all or that my wings would already be bare when they came in?"

He sighed and closed the book. "I suppose. Do you want me to examine them?"

"I would ask you to examine them... but I don't know how to control them yet. They happened sort of... randomly last night, after I volunteered at the skating rink."

Since yesterday, I had been trying to understand why I had gotten my wings now. And the only thing I had come up with is that volunteering and doing some good on Earth had caused it. Hell, it caused that man at the nursing home to see a halo over my head right before he died... but I still think that was just a hallucination.

DESTINY DIESS

"Have you been hallucinating?" Dr. Xiexie asked.

"No," I said, shaking my head. "But now and then I feel that *innate* urge to destroy like Javier did... but I haven't heard him."

Dr. Xiexie nodded. "You will feel that. It's likely, seeing you're half-angel, that feeling won't go away entirely for a long time... maybe not at all. Those hallucinations are mechanisms to corrupt pureness. You will struggle, but you must resist it."

"I will," I said, standing up to leave.

Before I could open the door, he cleared his throat. "And, Commander, there are only a few more days until the Crowning Ceremony... I suggest you spend them with your friends. Try to gather your goodness, because you don't want to lose control during the ceremony. You need to be strong."

CHAPTER 27

On my way back to Lust, I felt anxious. Not about my angel, but about that Envy. He hadn't been in the waiting room when I left Dr. Xiexie's office, but I didn't know if I reacted the way I should've. I wanted to be strong, but I didn't want to kill the man...

Even though Lucifer told me I could control my power, if I wanted, I didn't know what would happen if I didn't want to control it. That man wanted me to kill him to prove myself. If I killed him... would I lose control? What if I couldn't stop killing once I started?

I stepped through the portal into Lust, nodded at the guards who smiled at me, and walked out into the pink sunlight, letting the sun warm my frozen toes. I kept my head down, staring at the white stone walkway that led to the castle.

How could I show my people I was as strong, possibly even stronger than Asmodeus? While Eros believed it and Lucifer believed it and *I* was starting to believe it now too... not everyone else did.

Make them fear you.

Lucifer's words rang through my head. They sounded so

DESTINY DIESS

tempting, almost *too* tempting to pass up. "Make them fear me," I whispered to myself. I didn't want my people to fear me, but—

"Always getting in my fuckin' way," someone said in front of me. I stopped and glanced up to meet the alluring red eyes of that same Wrath I had been seeing everywhere. His muscles swelled under Lust's sun, his tail curling around his body.

"Always in my kingdom, Wrath." I stood in the middle of the walkway and pressed my lips together so he couldn't get by. Well, he could get by. All he'd have to do is step over into the grass and scoot by me, but I knew he wouldn't.

He sneered at me. "I can be wherever the fuck I want, *Commander.*"

I raised a brow at him and stepped closer, refusing to be intimidated by him. Though many things scared me in this unfamiliar world, he didn't. And something about it made me confident in myself and my abilities.

His barbed tail wrapped around my ankle, slid up my leg, and curled around my thigh. I took a deep breath, trying to ignore the tingles running up my inner thigh. I was positive I had never met this man before, but his touch felt so familiar.

"Are you the one stirring up trouble in my kingdom?" I asked through clenched teeth.

He chuckled, his eyes turning a brighter shade of red. "And if I am, what is Asmoedus's human daughter going to do about it?"

Before I could stop myself, I wrapped my hand around his throat and squeezed, pleasure rushing through my body. He grabbed my *wrist*, his claws digging into my skin, and I stumbled back.

Not in fear, but in realization.

"Oh, my god..." I whispered. This Wrath had touched me there before. I could feel his fingers, burned into my skin and my memory forever. I snatched my hand away. "You..." I took a deep breath, gazing him up and down.

I went to step back, but his tail tightened around my leg and

DEMONIC DESIRES

snaked further and further up my thigh, lingering in places that it shouldn't. "You were inside of Trevon, weren't you?" I asked. "You were the demon that was exorcised."

His eyes turned a lighter shade of red, the intensity in them not as strong as before. "That was his name?" he asked, lips curled into an evil smirk. "Trevon?"

Around us, the pink cherry blossoms shook slightly from the wind. My jaw twitched, and I clenched my fists, wanting to kill that man... but I held myself back. If I killed another Wrath, took their soul, and let it become part of me... there was no turning back. I'd have two demons destroying my mind, and I'd probably lose everything good in me.

Mom would be disappointed.

He gazed at me with those same eyes that Trevon had given me, yet they were softer this time. He stepped closer to me. I tried to step back again, but his tail forced me to stay still. "Trevon was weak. Weaker than I thought he'd be. I was glad you called that damn woman over. She was a real good kill, helped me return to who I truly am."

I pressed my lips together, nostrils flaring. "What's your damn problem?"

"My problem is that... everyone I do dirty work for wants you dead and I..." He paused for a moment. "But since I had been inside of Trevon and felt the way he felt about you... I can't fucking do it."

He couldn't kill me? He... felt the way Trevon felt about me? I didn't know what to think or even say, so I ignored that subtle sentence and asked, "Who do you work for now?"

"Are you that fuckin' stupid?" the Wrath asked, gazing down at me and shaking his head. He curled his finger around a strand of my hair, and I slapped it away, *my* wrath building inside of me. "Haven't you heard the rumors?"

My eyes widened even more, another wave of realization washing over me. "You're Biast, aren't you?" I whispered.

DESTINY DIESS

He uncurled his tail, released me, and pushed past me, walking toward the portal. I straightened myself out and gazed back at his large, departing figure. From his horns to his tail to that slick wrathful aura coming off of him, something about him screamed trouble. And I loved trouble.

"Why don't you do it?" I asked. "Why don't you try to kill me?"

"Because I'm sick of doing the dirty work. I have other plans with you." He glanced back at me, his lips curled into a smirk. "I'll see you at the ceremony, *Commander*."

CHAPTER 28

*B*iast didn't leave my mind all day. I sulked around the castle, waiting for Eros to come home and thinking about what he had said to me... that *he* had other plans for me. Was that why he hadn't tried to kill me yet? What were his plans? He had known exactly who I was this whole time, but hadn't laid a finger on me.

I pressed my lips together, walked down a set of stairs—deciding not to go to the kitchen and the bar area where Jasmine's scent lingered—and pushed my office door open. My body relaxed against Dad's comfy leather chair, and I opened his journal. If I was going to sulk, I was going to have to sulk and be somewhat productive.

Flipping aimlessly through Dad's journal, I stopped when I reached the prophecy page.

> *Three demons will rise from the ashes:*
> *The Devil, The Beast, The False Prophet.*
> *God will call them the Triad of Sinners,*
> *We will call them the Unholy Trinity.*
> *Under them, Hell will rule the Earths,*

And Heaven will fall to ruin.

The prophecy had been lingering in the back of my mind for days now. When would the beginning of the end officially start? When would we see the three most powerful demons rise from the ashes? How many bodies would fall? How much blood would be spilt? Would it be lies and betrayal or envy and wrath that leads us astray?

I had so many questions, and no answers.

After sighing, I brushed my fingers against the bottom of the page. When my ring grazed against it, black *Demoniac* letters appeared in the once blank space. My eyes widened, and I took off my ring, scrubbing the metallic side against the sheet until it had all filled with the demonic text.

There was more to the prophecy than Dad had wanted other people to discover.

But I couldn't read any of it. So, I hurried to the library, found all the books on how to speak *Demoniac*, and buried my face in each one for the next two hours. It didn't take long to figure out how to speak; I found myself mouthing the unfamiliar words as I read them. Sounds that I didn't even know I could make tumbled out of my mouth, almost naturally.

I glanced at Dad's journal, brows furrowed, and continued to read it almost as easily as I could read English. "Belial lives to speak more to the Commanders," I said aloud.

On the eighteenth day of the twenty-fifth year of the century, when the bodies are littered around the Devil and the blood has been drunk by the Beast and the lives have been bound to the False Prophet, the End will commence.

My eyes widened. It was the twenty-fifth year of this century, and the eighteenth day... was... when I'd be announced as Queen of Lust. I swallowed hard and slammed the book closed. This changed everything. There would be pure chaos during my ceremony, pure and utter chaos.

When I heard the palace door open, I sprinted down the stairs to find Eros. I needed to tell him about this *and* Biast now. I wouldn't be a fool and keep this from him like I had kept Javier.

The bar was filled with more people than usual, higher ranked Lusts from other towns, who were here for the ceremony. Eros was sitting in front of Jasmine at the bar and waiting for her to pour him a Passion Delight.

Jasmine locked eyes with me and smiled, that lustful glint on her face. I slid onto the seat next to Eros, inhaling his cinnamon scent. "There are more people than usual here tonight," I said.

Eros placed his hand on my knee, his fingers rubbing small circles on my inner thigh where Biast's tail was earlier. "There will be more people joining us in the palace these next couple of days. People from all over Lust—not just Chastion—are coming in for your crowning. Some people from Pride, as well."

"Lucifer?" I asked, brow raised.

"You know he'll be here," he said to me. "He'll be staying at the palace tomorrow night, after the pre-ceremonial party. There you'll announce your court and all the people who will take part in the ceremony. Then the Crowning is on the following day. Parts of the palace will be under construction until then. The Courting Pit will be outside in the Gardens, and then the court and the other commanders will bear witness to the Crowning in the Throne Room."

"Is Biast going to be there?"

"Unfortunately," Eros said, sipping his drink. "There isn't much I can do about it. It's law that every commander and their heirs must attend the Crowning of a new commander."

I nodded my head, staying quiet. "I saw him today."

Eros tensed, pulled his hand away from me, and sat up in his chair. "What do you mean you saw him?"

DESTINY DIESS

"I've been running into him a lot lately... I just didn't know who he was until today."

Eros's eyes filled with darkness, his sharp jaw tightening. "Has he laid a hand on you?"

Well, not in the *I'm-going-to-kill-you* way but I could still feel his tail wrapped tightly around my inner thigh, crawling up my leg, making me shiver. I inhaled Eros's scent, so I wouldn't have any *rash* thoughts, and shook my head. "He hasn't... but I've met him before."

A throaty growl escaped Eros's lips, and some people glanced over. "Where?"

"Remember, I told you Trevon was possessed by a demon more than once?" I kicked my legs back and forth. "Well... that was Biast."

"Biast was in your fucking home?" Eros asked, his fingers turning white on his glass. "I'm going to fuckin—"

I grabbed his hand and shook my head. "No. You're not going to do anything. I want him dead and gone just as much as you do... but we'll wait until after the Crowning. This will just cause a bigger fuss than what there is already."

"But—"

"No," I said sternly, leaving no room for an argument. I didn't want everyone to think I needed Eros to do *my* dirty work. That would make me look weak. I needed faith in the people. I needed them to trust me. I needed to be strong. And, as Biast said, he wasn't going to do anyone else's dirty work. He had other plans for me. But by the way, he spoke earlier, I didn't think he'd hurt me. And if he tried, I'd kill him like I killed his brother.

"We have other things to talk about," I said in a hushed tone. "Like how the Beginning of the End will commence on the day of my crowning." He furrowed his brows at me and parted his lips to speak, but I just shook my head and said, "Just prepare," because *I* didn't know what the Unholy Trinity meant for us either.

156

CHAPTER 29

"You think Zane will like this on me?" Maria asked from Dr. U's bathroom. We were supposed to be here to help Dr. U get ready for her date, but it turned into all of us preparing for something. Zane had asked Maria to the pre-ceremonial party tonight. Dr. U was about to go on her first date in years. And all I was trying to do was impress my Eros for the party tonight—hoping that it wouldn't go as terribly as the last one in Lust did.

"Come on out, Maria," Dr. U said, moving her lips as I tried so desperately to put a light pink coat of lipstick on them. I had begged her to let me try a bold look on her, but she denied. Dr. U peered over my shoulder from the couch at Maria, made the funniest pained face I had ever seen, and smiled.

I suppressed a giggle and turned around to see Maria in a very unflattering pink ball gown. Ruffles and glitter and even small rose flowers sewn into the train. Maria placed her hand on her hip. "Yeah, I know. I don't like it either. Zane brought it over this morning and told me I'd look good in it."

"Maria," I said. "If you're going to attend a party in Lust, you got to show some skin."

DESTINY DIESS

"I literally have nothing else to wear. All my dresses are flirty, but I don't have anything for a queen's ball!" She took a deep breath, gazing at the ground. "You know what? I'll just put on some mascara, take a couple shots, and go in this damn dress. I don't have time."

Dr. U stood up. "Wait here, Maria. I have something that might fit you." She disappeared into the hall, her footsteps becoming quieter and quieter.

Maria collapsed onto the couch next to me, angrily grabbing a cracker from the coffee table that Dr. U had put out for us for snacks. "I love Dr. U... but do you really think she's going to have something for me to wear?" she asked. "Can I try something of yours on, if I don't like it?"

"You can try, but..." I gazed out the Palladian window and into the forest that surrounded Dr. U's house. "You won't fit into anything of mine. You're a lot skinnier than I am."

She signed and slouched back onto the blue couch. "You think that's why Zane doesn't want to date me?" she asked, brows furrowed together. "I don't have enough for him?"

I raised my brows. "No! Maria, where'd you get that from?"

"Well..." She paused and shrugged her shoulders. "I don't know. Sex demons seem to have a type..." She let out a quiet laugh. "You."

I gave her an *Are-you-serious?* look, and she bumped her shoulder into mine. "I'm just kidding, but seriously... I was just starting to get comfortable with the idea of being a couple, but, whenever I ask him about it, he always steers the conversation elsewhere."

"A couple? I thought you didn't want to date him because he wanted an open relationship," I said. She made a face and groaned, rolling her bright blue eyes. I grabbed her hands. "Maria, you need a lot of trust in an open-relationship."

"How do you do it?" she whispered.

"I don't." My lips curled into a smirk. "As far as I know, Eros

158

doesn't do anything with anyone else." But I was getting awfully suspicious of him and Luci. "He's demisexual, I think."

"Huh?" she asked, brow raised.

"He only enjoys having sex with someone he has formed an emotional relationship with."

"Oh." Her frown deepened. "How does he feel when you flirt with other people?"

"Well..." I started, thinking about all the times Eros has gotten off on the thought of me sleeping with Lucifer or flirting with someone else. It was one of his kinks, and I didn't mind it—as long as he really wanted to watch. I shook my head at her. "Nevermind that. Every demon is different. If you want to ask Eros about it, you can at the party tonight."

Dr. U walked back into the room with a gorgeous black silky dress. "Maria, I found this."

Maria stood up, her eyes wide. "Oh, my god."

"Where were you keeping this?" I asked, drawing my fingers against the silky material. It looked like it would fit right to Maria's body, cling to every one of her curves.

"I wore it once... in my Kasey-days." Dr. U smiled.

Maria squealed, took the dress, and hurried back into the bathroom to change into it. Dr. U sat back down on the couch with me and grabbed another stick of lipstick from the table, a darker matte pink. She grasped my jaw lightly. "Your turn."

I closed my eyes, letting her apply the lipstick and trying not to smile. This was the first time, in a long time, we had spent time together. I had learned so much about her within the past few days compared to all the time she had raised me.

She smelt faintly like Ollie's, and I wondered if Kasey and her used to go there. Did they have cute breakfasts together? Feed each other strawberries? Listen to sweet love songs in the car in the pouring rain? Did Dr. U miss her as much as I did?

Dr. U glided the lipstick across my lips, and I blew a deep breath out of my nose. The subtle action reminded me of when

DESTINY DIESS

she helped me get ready for all of my dance recitals when I was younger, all the times she watched me in my pink tutu twirl around the stage, everything a mother would do.

"Do you think I'll make a good queen?" I asked.

"Dani," she said softly. "You'll be a great queen."

I opened my eyes, letting them fill with tears. "You really think so?"

She nodded her head and smiled at me. "Of course. You're sweet and loving and caring. You follow your heart and do what you think is best. Whether they like you as a queen matters, but how you love yourself matters more." She grabbed my hands. "I don't know much about demons. I only spent a few weeks with Kasey... so all I can tell you is to stay true to who you are. Don't let the darkness consume you, and if you do... make sure you have someone who can bring you back to the light."

A tear slid down my cheek, and Dr. U pushed it away, smiling even wider at me. I tilted my head into her hand and smiled. I had compared Dr. U to Mom so much, but... I should've. She and Mom both wanted the same things from me—to see me happy and smiling, and I appreciated her more than anything.

Suddenly Maria let out a scream from the bathroom, followed by an "It's perfect!"

Dr. U drew me closer to her, and we laughed. This life—no matter the struggles I had been through or would face soon—was perfect in its own imperfect way.

CHAPTER 30

*M*aria and I gazed into a window at Crimson's Nouveau, watching Dr. U sit at the bar with the pretty, pink-haired beauty. In the crowded restaurant, they laughed over drinks before a hostess ushered them to a booth.

I grinned and grabbed Maria's hand, leading her to the alley behind the restaurant. My heart warmed, butterflies fluttering in my stomach. "I hope she has a good time tonight. Dr. U deserves it."

Some flurries drifted down from the grey sky, and I nodded to Zial, one of the guards near The Lounge who always opened portals to Hell for me. After moving his hands in a pattern I hadn't quite picked up on yet and tossing a lit match onto the ground, a black mist formed in the alleyway.

Maria stared at it with wide eyes, then walked up to it—thrusting out her fingers and watching them disappear into the portal. "Last time I went into one of these things, Zane made me close my eyes. What's in here?"

After clutching her hand in mine, I said, "You don't want to know, Maria." I knew for a fact that it'd give her nightmares. Hell,

DESTINY DIESS

it still gave me the chills seeing my best friend, my ex-boyfriend, and my mother doing those unholy things. "Close your eyes and don't open them until I tell you."

She arched a brow at me, but I arched mine harder. She sighed and closed her eyes, letting the gusts of wind from the portal plaster her dress to her petite body. I thanked Zial and pulled Maria into the portal, hoping that she'd listen to me.

Though I had been in the portal about a hundred times since my first, the demons in there still freaked me out a bit. My fingers dug into Maria's shoulders as I pushed her toward the light pink path toward Lust. Demons reached out for her, sensing her quickened heart rate, but I refused to let them have her.

When we finally reached the portal, I pressed my hands into her back, told her to brace herself, and pushed her through it. She almost somersaulted through the air, but my personal guard, Esha, caught her arm and lifted her to her feet.

Maria smiled at her, cheeks flushing red, and readjusted her dress, so her breasts weren't falling out of it anymore. I walked through the portal and nodded to Esha. "Is everything okay?"

"Yes, Commander. Eros wanted me to be here when you arrived."

My lips curled into a smile, thinking about Eros and how hard he had worked to make tonight perfect. But all I knew was that tonight might be the last perfect night for a long time, if Belial's prophecy was true and the Unholy Trinity would begin their rise tomorrow during my ceremony.

Pink petals from the cherry blossoms littered the white stone walkways. Demons, dressed in their most sultry silk clothing, walked toward the palace, laughing with their friends. Esha followed us toward the palace, glancing at Maria every so often.

"I should tell you that Trevon, your ex-boyfriend, is here upon Eros's request," Esha said, finally breaking the silence. My brows raised. Eros asked Trevon to come after what he had done the other night? Esha stared up at the palace, gazing at the long line to get in. "He told me it was for his safety, since Zane can't watch him tonight."

I slowly nodded my head, wondering if that really was the reason. Sometimes Eros's reasoning wasn't always what he made it out to be. We walked alongside the line to the front doors and into the castle.

The lobby was bustling with people, dancing and flirting with each other. The sweet scent of Passion Delight lingered heavily in the air. I glanced around the room, locking eyes with Eros who stood near the platters of Fervor Crisps with Lucifer.

Brown hair parted to one side, a strand curling onto his forehead, those devilish eyes staring at Luci. I glanced at them for a moment longer, feeling that lingering ache in my core and reminiscing on the memory of the other night when they had kissed. His plump lips curled into a soft smile, and I smiled at him, my heart feeling full. While it was erotic and so damn sexy, something about it seemed so intimate.

Maria gazed around with me, finding Zane standing by the bar and getting his drink mixed by Jasmine. My gaze flickered to her, tongue sliding against my fangs. Tonight would be glorious, before Hell turned upside down.

Esha and I followed an eager Maria to the bar. She placed her palms on Zane's shoulders and squeezed lightly. Zane turned around, inhaling sharply. His eyes widened, pupils dilating, when he saw Maria in her tight, little dress. "You're not wearing the dress I got you," he said to her, but I could tell that he didn't mind. Not. At. All.

Jasmine pushed two Passion Delights across the bar, and I grabbed one. "She couldn't wear that thing," I said. "It wasn't anything that one of the commander's friends would wear." I grabbed Maria's hand and twirled her in a circle. "And, besides, doesn't this look good on her?"

DESTINY DIESS

Zane stood, wrapping his arms around Maria's small waist. "Good?" he asked. He mumbled something inaudible against her lips, and Maria's cheeks turned bright pink. When she giggled into his chest, he took her hand and his Passion Delight and tugged her toward the Triad who sat on a couple couches near the far end of the room.

"Watch her," I said to Esha. "Don't let anyone hurt her." Esha nodded her head and walked toward them, keeping her distance but watching Maria.

I sipped my drink, placed my forearms on the bar, and leaned forward, watching Jasmine take care of some demons. Unlike the other morning, she was dressed in her usual little black dress. It came to her mid-thigh and dipped along the chest line all the way to her abdomen, showing off so much skin that it made me want to—

"Do you like my new uniform?" she asked, twirling in a circle and walking toward me.

I sucked in a deep breath, smelling *her*, and slid onto a seat. "I do."

"What do you like about it, Commander?"

After taking another sip of my drink, I swallowed hard. What did I like about it? God, I liked a lot about it. I smirked at her. "That you're in it," I said, feeling the warmth in my core.

She leaned against the bar, placing her elbows on the counter and pressing her breasts together. "What else?" she asked, face inches from mine.

My heart raced in my chest, and I could smell the sweet scent of cinnamon drifting through my nostrils. I inhaled and stared into her intense eyes. "I like the way it fits on you," I said, brushing my finger against the neckline of her dress. "The way it plunges between your breasts..." I ran my finger down it, fingers brushing lightly again her breasts. "The way you get goosebumps when I touch you in it," I whispered.

164

For the first time, her cheeks flushed. I sipped my drink, feeling the liquor courage pumping through my veins, and stood. "Do you like mine?" I asked, trailing my hands down my sides to my waist.

"It's beautiful."

"What do *you* like about it?" I asked with a smile, throwing her words back at her.

"What's not to love about it?" Eros asked in my ear. His arms wrapped around my waist, and he placed a lingering kiss on my neck. He gazed up at Jasmine and smirked against me. "Isn't that right, Jasmine?"

Jasmine smiled and nodded her head, not daring to say a word in front of Eros, like usual. I arched a brow at her. "What do you like about it, Jasmine?" I asked her again, wanting her to answer me. Something about finally having the upper hand against her made me *excited.*

Eros trailed his hand over my breast and squeezed. "Do you like this?" he asked Jasmine. Jasmine leaned further against the bar, watching us, and nodded her head. Eros trailed his fingers down my body to my hips, gripping my ass in his hand. "This?"

Jasmine sucked in a deep breath, and Eros's hand traveled even lower to the high-slit in my dress. "What about this?" he asked, slipping his hand under the material and brushing it against my underwear. I clenched, a wave of heat warming my core.

Eros rubbed his fingers in small circles around my clit. I grasped his hand, but he pushed it away. "Let me touch you," he said, wrapping his other hand around the front of my neck and kissing my jaw.

I stared at Jasmine, watching her watch Eros from across the bar. Her legs crossed, her eyes hazy, her scent so damn strong. "She wants to touch you, Dani," Eros whispered into my ear. He pressed his hardness against my backside, and I clenched.

God, I bet he wanted to watch her touch me too. I licked my lips, staring at Jasmine and trying so hard to control myself. Earlier, I promised that I wouldn't go into the Lust Rooms until later tonight when I knew this party would go smoothly.

After gathering all the goddamn self-control I had, I leaned across the bar, placed my drink right in front of her, and said, "Maybe later, I'll take you up on your offer." Then I walked away from them and back into the crowd, deciding that it would be a good idea to find Trevon, the one damn man I wasn't attracted to anymore, and hoped it'd calm me down.

But I didn't know if anything could calm me down at this point. All I could think about was what I had promised Jasmine. It would be the first time I had ever even thought about being with another woman, and while part of me was hesitant, the other part of me wanted it.

From across the room, Trevon stood by the Fervor Crisps, picked one up, and broke it into two pieces, stuffing one in his mouth. I pushed through a few people to reach him and Maeve who were talking.

"You've both met already," I said with a smile, cutting into their conversation.

"Dani," Trevon said with a smile. He went in for a hug, but I stepped away, not wanting to feel uncomfortable again. Trevon looked pissed for a moment, then he turned back to the Fervor Crisp. "Maeve and I had met before. She's one of Samantha's friends."

Maeve almost choked on her pastry. "No, I'm not." She scrunched her nose in disgust and shot me a *I-don't-know-where-that-came-from* look. "I've met her a few times in passing. She used to be part of my friend group on Earth, but..." She shivered, as if thinking back to a terrible memory, and leaned close to me. "She was always so jealous, and that's coming from an Envy."

God, did I already know that Samantha was a jealous woman.

I glanced at Trevon. "How is Samantha doing?"

DEMONIC DESIRES

After stuffing the other half of the crisp into his mouth, he shrugged. "Haven't seen her."

Trevon hadn't seen the one woman hell-bent on getting with him? My stomach tightened, an uneasy feeling forming. But... for tonight... I pushed the thought away. She'd be another problem I would deal with tomorrow.

CHAPTER 31

"There you are," Lucifer said about an hour into the party. Everything had been going surprisingly well—so well that I was getting suspicious of someone saying something and ruining all the fun.

Maeve bowed her head to Luci, a strand of her blonde hair falling into her face. Trevon rolled his eyes, not even sparing Lucifer a glance as Luci curled his arm around mine and tugged on it gently. "I'm going to steal Dani away for a bit. She has to make some announcements."

When Lucifer pulled me away, Maeve and Trevon fell back into an easy conversation. I gazed back at Maeve, not in jealousy but in curiosity. She and Trevon seemed to get along very, very well. Maybe... they'd be good together. It'd get Trevon off my back and a demon like her might keep him satisfied. Maybe she'd stop all the jealousy he had for Eros.

"I hope you've chosen your court," he said to me. Before I answered him, Lucifer cleared his throat, and everyone stopped talking—almost immediately. I glanced up at him with wide-eyes at the complete control he commanded just by his voice alone.

One day, *I* wanted to have that kind of power. *I wanted to be able* to control hundreds of demons just by speaking a single word. That was power in its rawest, simplest form.

"As leader of the strongest kingdom and one of the first fallen angels," Lucifer started, gesturing around the room filled with demons. "I have the honor of introducing the new soon-to-be Commander of Lust."

I stared around at some demons I'd met in Chastion, like the Triad and even Annen who was in the back smiling widely at me.

"Dani will announce her court for tomorrow afternoon," Lucifer said, placing a hand on my shoulder and squeezing tightly. He pulled me toward him and leaned down only slightly to whisper in my ear. "Remember what I told you, Dani."

After taking a deep breath, I stepped forward and placed my hands by my side. "Tomorrow, I will become Queen of Lust, and while all of you will watch the Courting Pit and my Crowning Ceremony, I can only allow a select few by my side and into the Pit, if someone wants to challenge me for my rightful place."

That weird and awkward part of me wanted to make a joke to lighten the mood because big crowds of people really weren't my cup of Passion Delight, but I pressed my lips together and saved that for when I was with Eros.

"The Commanders, the Lords and Ladies, the heirs to the throne and their siblings of each kingdom will all be there, as tradition states, to take part in the Pit—if needed—and to watch the Crowning. For my court, I have selected..." I took a deep breath and smiled. "Eros..."

Eros stared at me from across the room, his devilish green eyes filling with excitement.

"The Triad," I said. Axel gave Enji a *fuck-yeah-we-get-pussy* look, while Zane just stared directly at me like he had been for days now. I raised my brow. Maybe that wasn't the best decision of my life, but... we'd see.

"Jasmine." She waved at me from across the bar, lips in a small, seductive smile, her tongue sliding across her lower lip. I smiled back, then looked at Maeve who stood alone by the Fervor Crisps. "And Maeve."

"Are you fucking kidding me?" someone said from across the room. Everyone turned around, heads snapping toward the door. Heels clacked against the granite floors, and demons parted the way for someone to walk.

My eyes widened when I saw Kasey emerge from the crowd, a sleek black silk dress clinging to her body and pearl earrings hanging from her ears. She had a scowl on her face, and her eyes were a bright green.

I glanced at Eros who looked just as confused as I was. Lucifer chuckled from beside me and sipped his drink. "Finally. Something to lighten this party up."

After giving him a side-eye, I glanced back at Kasey. She marched right up to Lucifer and me, pursed her blood-red lips, and swung her high ponytail around to her shoulder. Eros hurried through the crowd, snatching her by her wrist, but she pulled it away.

"What are you doing?" she asked me. "Letting Maeve into your court? Inviting her here?" Her eyes glowed brighter than they already were. Maeve wove through the crowd until she stood by my side, brows furrowed in worry. Kasey stared right at her. "You shouldn't be at this party."

Before Maeve could say anything, I stepped in front of a towering Kasey and glared at her, trying hard to keep Javier from rattling my insides. "She has every right to be here because I invited her."

"Do you know who she is?" Kasey asked, jaw twitching. She took another threatening step forward, trying so hard to intimidate me. And while I thought she was intimidating at one point... she didn't scare me now.

DEMONIC DESIRES

"I didn't invite you, Kasey." I pressed my lips together. *"You shouldn't be here."*

"Maeve is from one of Envy's most schemeful families. They take everything from people. Is that really who you're going to choose to be in your court instead of *me."*

And while I thought her outburst was all because she wanted to be friends with me again, her last few words proved that this was all for herself.

She was envious. Of me.

Maeve stepped closer to me, almost visibly shaking in fear. Though her eyes were usually an intense green, they were soft now. And it scared the living hell out of me to see her look so... broken. Maeve had always been strong, but now she looked so weak. "She's lying, Dani. She doesn't want you to have any friends other than her."

Eros glanced at me, and I stared back at him, wanting nothing more than to tell him to get her out. She was ruining the entire party, my one night before the damn chaos began.

Kasey shook in rage. "Maeve is bad news. You can't blindly trust Envies."

I stepped forward, something inside of me snapping. "You're right," I said to her, clenching my fists by my side. Eros stepped closer to me, but I held my hand up at him. "Don't, Eros." I was finally going to give her a piece of my mind and, unlike on Earth, I would not hold back this time.

Kasey pursed her lips at me. It was a subtle, Envy action. And it enraged me.

"I shouldn't have trusted you," I said. She was an Envy. She hurt me over and over, and I let her. It was stupid and rash and weak of me to do, but I learned my lesson. I wouldn't trust people like her again, people who switched up on me in a moment's notice.

She flared her nostrils. "Are you serious, Dani? Are you that fucking blind? She's a monster. She will hurt you. She's—"

171

DESTINY DIESS

"You're just envious of Dani," Maeve interrupted, standing by my side, that strong expression back on her face. "You're jealous that she will sit on the throne that your mother always wanted."

My brows softened, and for a moment everything made perfect sense. It was Kasey stirring up trouble around Lust; she was the one spreading rumors about me not being strong enough to rule the kingdom.

Every part of my body hurt in betrayal, but Dad had told me that betrayal was coming, so I should've been prepared for it. I swallowed my hurt and steadied my voice. "Is that what this is?" I asked. "Are you trying to make a claim to my throne that my father had sat on for thousands and thousands of years?"

"I am a lot of things," Kasey said. "But I am not envious of you." She stepped closer to me, and for a moment her features softened. "I just want the best for you."

"The best place for me is on the throne."

Her lips twitched, and that anger re-appeared in her eyes. "You humans joke about Hell like it's nothing... but it's shitty down here sometimes. People will try to kill you. You won't be able to handle it, Dani. You can barely handle me gone."

I growled at her. Not only did she not believe in me, but she was embarrassing me in front of all the other commanders. She thought I would be a terrible leader and that someone else deserved to lead the kingdom.

"Don't fucking tell me I won't be a good commander. I will take anybody's soul who tries to take my throne, rip off their horns, and mount them on the fucking wall. The throne is mine, like it was my father's. I will not let anyone tell me otherwise. And if you want a fucking war, then I'll give you one." I balled my hands into fists. "Take her to The Chains."

Kasey widened her eyes, acting as if she was surprised that I had so much confidence. But I was fed up with her and her lies. "You can't do that. I have to attend the ceremony tomorrow; I'm a sibling to the heir."

DEMONIC DESIRES

"No," I said. "You're not. Your mother is dead. Your father is dead. You have no claim to any throne, especially one that isn't yours." I clenched my jaw. "Now, take her away before I have to do it myself."

CHAPTER 32

*A*fter Esha escorted Kasey to the portal, people at the party slowly started to leave. One by one, they all downed their Passion Delights, muttered some farewells to me, and hurried toward the palace doors. I frowned at their departing figures, trying so hard not to shed a tear.

It wasn't fair how Kasey could come in and ruin this all for me. It wasn't fair that she had been the one who stirred up trouble around Lust. She was supposed to support me, not hurt me.

Maeve wrapped her arm around my waist and rested her chin on my shoulder, her sweet scent of lavender drifting into my nostrils. "Are you okay?"

I gently pushed her away. "I just want to be alone right now," I said, jaw twitching. Though this whole situation made me an emotional wreck, I could just feel my wrath bubbling inside of me. I didn't want to freak out on anyone. I just wanted to relax. "Please, go."

She frowned at me, then nodded her head, walking toward the palace doors without making a fuss about it like Kasey did. I wanted to stop her and ask her if *she* was okay after

DEMONIC DESIRES

that, but I felt like I would snap into a bunch of tiny little pieces.

Only a few people lingered by the bar, and I stared around at the now great yet barren room. I grabbed a Passion Delight from a random table—not giving a damn whose it was—and threw it back, letting it slide down my throat.

Without letting another negative thought haunt my mind, I walked to the bar and stood between Eros and Lucifer. Jasmine took my cup and asked if I wanted another one, but I rudely ignored her, knowing that Javier was about to snap. "Is everyone gone?" I asked Eros. "Did Maria get back safe with Zane?"

"Left about twenty minutes ago."

"Did Trevon leave with them?"

Eros paused for a second, his green eyes widening. "No, I thought he left already. I hadn't seen him since you and Maeve were talking to him."

Damn it.

My heart almost dropped. Now Trevon was missing. The vein in my neck pulsed violently, and I dug my claws straight through the metal bar counter. If someone took him to get back at me... If it was Biast, I swear I would rip his head off.

"Someone was supposed to be fucking watching him." I growled, a red film blurring my vision for only a moment. "Why the fuck didn't that happen?" Pure rage was pumping through my body, and I knew that it wasn't Eros's fault...

But Trevon didn't deserve to be in any more demon drama.

"Calm down," Lucifer said, loosening his tie and knocking back some Vemon. "He's probably walking around your palace."

Calm down? I couldn't calm down. Not after what had happened last time. Not after Biast's promise to me. I stormed through the castle, shouting Trevon's name and trying to find any fucking sign of where he could've gone.What was I going to do if he was gone? I couldn't have him lost somewhere in the pits of Hell and continue with my Crowning Ceremony.

175

DESTINY DIESS

After searching the bottom floor and finding nothing, I hurried up a flight of stairs and looked through every single one of the rooms, my heels digging into the red carpets. Dim white lights hung from the ceiling every few feet; the doors were all closed; the hallways smelt like vanilla and cinnamon. Nothing seemed out of place, except that there weren't any guards on duty on this floor.

There were always guards on duty. Someone must've led them away.

I sprinted into each room like a wild animal, ripping the closet doors open, trying to sense someone's soul, suppressing my rage... at least, trying to. Javier had been quiet for far too long and was about to burst.

Another room. Another let down.

My eyes locked on to the last room: my office. I pushed the door open and let out a wrathful shriek. Sitting on my chair, Trevon was clawing at the lock on my father's journal, trying to rip it off with his teeth.

"What the hell are you doing?"

The binds were ripping, the tattered leather becoming more and more destroyed with every tooth mark. I snatched it from him, and he latched his teeth into my forearm instead, immediately drawing blood.

I screamed, feeling the blood in my eyes, begging me to release Javier and end his life. My vision blurred for a moment, and I stumbled back—terrified of what would happen if I surrendered to this innate urge.

Trevon curled his lips into an ugly snarl, his eyes flashing... green. I backed away from him, my heart beating hard against my chest. Calm yourself, Dani. Stay calm. I grasped Mom and Dad's ring, brushing my thumb over the pendant. "Eros!" I shouted. "Get in here now!"

Trevon's nails lengthened into claws, and he stepped toward

me. Trevon was still there somewhere. Whoever had possessed him this time didn't control him fully. I could see the faintest struggle in his eyes.

He reached for the journal, his claws digging into my skin this time. So damn deep that I swore he cut the muscle. I grasped my arm and stared down at it, watching the blood seep from my forearm and onto the ground. I inhaled the scent and sucked the cut into my mouth.

"Blood," Javier whispered. "Need to drink blood."

My eyes closed in utter bliss at the taste of blood, the journal slipping from my hands. Ecstasy rushed through me, and I shuddered in pleasure, drinking more and more of it until my cut had healed. And, even then, I leaned back against the wall and sighed in relief. My mind was fuzzy, my vision blurred.

Cinnamon entered the room—another tasty scent. I heard a loud crash and then a bang, and I blinked my eyes to see Eros standing above Trevon. My wooden bookcase toppled over from the impact and pieces of wood lodged in Trevon's flesh. Eros ripped something from him and tossed my journal back to me.

"Give that back to me!" Trevon said, immediately standing and reaching for the journal.

"What the fuck is wrong with you?" Eros said, sinking his claws into the back of Trevon's neck and holding him in the air. When Eros really looked at him, his eyes widened. "An... Envy?"

"Is it your sister?" I asked, licking the blood off my lips and hugging my journal to my chest. Esha had taken Kasey to The Chains, but that was before Trevon went missing. If it was Kasey, trying to find out all my damn secrets, I would lose it. I'd surrender to Javier and let him burn everything down in fucking flames. We would create our own Kingdom of Wrath right here in my palace.

Eros stared at him—trying to get a good read—but Trevon wouldn't look him in the eye, so Eros grabbed his chin and

DESTINY DIESS

forced him to look into his black pits. After a few moments, Eros growled and tightened the grip on his neck. "No."

I pressed my lips together. She probably hired an Envy to possess him right before my ceremony, so I looked weak and like I didn't know what I was doing. Had she planned this all along? Had she been trying to tear me down from the moment I met her?

"We are going to The Chains," I said, marching right out of the room and back downstairs. Lucifer and Jasmine were talking by the bar.

Luci smirked. "What's got you all angry?" He stood up, and I growled at him.

"I'm not in the fucking mood."

He stretched out his arms. "You should be having the night of your life tonight," he said. Eros stepped into the room, pushing a struggling Trevon in front of him. Lucifer raised his brow and sat back down. "Fair enough."

"We're going to The Chains," Eros told Lucifer. "We'll be back in a couple hours."

"Fun," Lucifer said, tipping his glass at me. "Tell all my friends there that Luci says hello."

After taking a deep breath, I snatched Trevon's ear and pulled him toward the palace doors. Tonight was going from bad to so fucking bad, it wasn't even funny. Out of all nights, why did it have to happen tonight? It could've happened tomorrow night or yesterday or, hell, right after the ceremony for all I cared. But... tonight?

People crowded the walkway toward the portal, coming from it and heading to Chastion in droves. They parted for us as I continued to storm around them—without stopping once. Eros walked beside me, his jaw clenched and his gaze trained on the people in front of us.

"This is absolutely ridiculous that we have to do this again," I said through clenched teeth. Eros opened the portal room door for me and Trevon. People sat on the velvet red couches, gossiping with each other. Guards were pushing people along to keep everything moving smoothly.

Esha hopped out of the portal, saw me, and said, "Kasey is locked away. Won't be bothering you, Commander." I nodded swiftly to her and shoved Trevon toward the portal. The guards stopped demons from entering and allowed us to pass.

I tried hard to not be rough with Trevon in the portal, but when we reached Pride, I physically couldn't help it. I shoved him right through it, watched him land hard on his stomach, and let out a laugh. Almost immediately, I slapped a hand over my mouth, unsure of where it had come from.

Deep down, I knew that this wasn't Trevon's fault. He was just susceptible to so much demon shit because Javier had messed with his head. But... Javier was also messing with mine and I couldn't help not feeling an ounce of shame or guilt for what I had just done.

And *that* scared me more than Kasey could ever hope to.

The guards in Pride nodded respectfully to me and opened the doors to Lucifer's white wonderland. Eros muttered an apology to them and ushered me down the damn cold path toward The Chains.

Snow fell around us, the sky an eerie grey—even this late at night. And when those pretty white flakes touched my skin, they immediately turned to water. My entire body felt like it was on fire, burning like the pits of Tartarus.

We trudged up a small hill, and I stared at Luci's castle and the glaciers-like cliffs that surrounded it. When we made it to the hilltop, I smiled at the ashy-grey building Eros called The Chains —heavily guarded by demons.

Trevon took one quick look at it and immediately trembled. His body convulsing back and forth, trying to steer me off the

DESTINY DIESS

path and into the snow. I tightened my grip until my claws sunk deep in his muscle. "Stop moving, Trevon."

"I'm not going back there, Dani!" he shrieked, fear clear in his eyes. It was *his* voice and *his* fear, not the demon's. And while part of me pitied him, I continued walking. Whoever Kasey hired would pay for ruining my damn party.

"You have to."

Tears... damn tears rolled down his cheeks, and he grasped my hand. "No, Dani, please. I'll do anything. I can't... can't deal with it again. I can still feel the demon clawing its way up my throat from last time."

I growled to quiet him down and nodded to the guards at the prison. When they opened the doors, Trevon struggled even more. The stench of feces rolled out of the building in waves. I scrunched my nose and stepped into the room, gazing at the hundreds of glowing colored eyes on me in the darkness.

Someone turned on the bright lights, the shuddering sound echoing through the large concrete room. Demons cowered back in their cages, shielding their eyes with their talons. I took a deep breath, visions of last time I was here haunting me.

Stacks of cages lined the walls and created narrow walkways around the room. I pushed Trevon toward the back and ignored all the vile questions like *"Back again?"* or *"Decided you wanted another taste of Hell?"*

One demon in a cage on the ground reached out his bloody hands and brushed his fingers across Trevon's shoulder. Trevon stumbled back into me, trembling even harder. "Don't be afraid of them," I said through clenched teeth. "They feed off of it."

"How am I not supposed to be terrified?" he asked, voice cracking. "They're fucking demons."

I pushed him down another narrow walkway, trying to avoid the feces on the ground, and locked eyes with Kasey. She sat in a cell toward the back, her tight dress clinging to her body, her head hung in shame, an actual tear rolling down her cheek. Half

180

of my angelic heart hurt for her. She didn't belong here. At least... I wanted to believe that.

When she sniffed the air and saw Eros and me, she stood up and grasped the silver bars, despite the natural bad reaction demons had to silver. "Dani, listen to me and what I have to say." But I didn't have to listen to anything she had to say. She betrayed me. She wanted me to hate Maeve—the only person who had been my friend the whole time I was here. I couldn't trust Kasey or listen to her, especially not when my throne was on the line and when there was this underlying threat of the Unholy Trinity ripping Heaven to pieces tomorrow.

I opened the cell across from hers and threw Trevon into it. He shook his head from side to side, grasping his throat already. "Dani... Dani, please, don't do this." He dropped to his knees, and I clasped a chain around his neck. "No! Dani!" he screamed, his brown eyes wide and filled with fear.

The Wrath demon who possessed Trevon last time sat in the cell Eros had put him in, biting into a severed human leg. He chuckled, his rage suppressed. "Back again, you fuckin' bastard?"

My head snapped in his direction, and I clenched my jaw. "Don't," I said with such intensity that his eyes widened and he became quiet. The entire damn room became silent, and it was oddly peaceful.

Too peaceful.

And, then, everyone bursted out in laughter. *"Daughter of Asmodeus thinks she's a big deal now that she's about to rule."*

"Heard that your kingdom will be taken from you tomorrow."

"Think you can intimidate demons when you're not even fully one yourself?"

I took a deep breath and stepped closer to Eros, my fingers brushing against his. Something about the soft touch made my heart race in a pleasant way. It calmed the raging Javier inside of me and helped me focus on Trevon whose lips were quivering.

Part of me felt bad for Trevon. Though he had fucked up in so

DESTINY DIESS

many ways, he didn't deserve this. He really didn't. But because he was friends with me, this kept happening to him. And I didn't want to cause anymore pain.

After struggling a few moments, his eyes shifted to an envious green color. He fell, belly-first, onto the ground, his body seizing back and forth, green foam spurting from his mouth. I struggled to watch it happen to him, but I watched the entire time. If he had to go through it, the least I could do is watch.

From the insides of his stomach, something moved around. Hands and fists and feet struggling to come out of him. Trevon grasped his waist, trying to hold it all in so he wouldn't burst. Then, suddenly, his chest cavity expanded. And then his throat— the demon curling into a large bowling-ball like sphere again. And then the beast clawed its way out of Trevon through his mouth.

Green blood gushed out of his mouth and down his chin. The demon leapt out toward me, claws ready to dig right into my eyes, but Eros caught it in his hands and clasped another chain around its neck. I grabbed Trevon's body before it could smack against the ground and slowly put him down, resting him on his side so he wouldn't choke on the blood.

I glanced up at the demon, and my eyes widened. Covered in Trevon's stomach acid, Samantha stood in front of me, struggling with her chains. What the actual hell was going on? Samantha was a damn Envy demon?

Jesus fucking Christ.

Samantha's eyes blazed a bright green. "I should've known you'd figure me out. You always have Trevon curled around your finger. You stupid fucking bitch!"

Calm, Dani, stay calm.

"What were you doing in my office? What were you trying to find?" I asked Samantha, but when she didn't respond, I turned on my heel and glared at Kasey. She hired the one person who tried to kill me—not once but *twice*.

182

DEMONIC DESIRES

Samantha cackled, and I ached to rip out her throat. I should've taken care of her the moment she spiked my drink... but I was weak then. I didn't know any better. I didn't think I could kill someone with just a kiss.

I knew better now.

All I wanted was to see her dead, but I wanted her to suffer. And I would see her suffer. After the ceremony tomorrow, I wanted to drown her in the Styx River. Let her float to Tartarus. Stick her on a post. Cut off her horns. Wear them like a fucking trophy.

Samantha threw her head back and stepped toward me, trying to intimidate me. The silver chains dug into her skin, hooking into it. "You think you're so high and mighty... Well, know this, Commander. Tomorrow you'll see your kingdom taken right from you by one of *my* kind."

I glanced at Kasey again, my heart pounding in my ears. She had to have hired more people to fuck with me. Kasey shook her head, looking so damn desperate. "Dani, I haven't hired anyone. I didn't do this."

Trevon lifted his head, wobbling from side to side, and rested himself against the bars. He mumbled something under his breath—words I had never heard spoken before by anyone other than Mom. It sounded like a hymn she'd sing to me whenever I accidentally fell off my bicycle and got hurt.

Samantha continued to say something, but I ignored her, listening to his harmonic humming. He opened his eyes for a moment, and I watched them turn from dull brown to... white. I took a step back and glanced at Eros who had seen it too.

Thankfully, nobody else saw Trevon's white eyes as they were all too bothered by trying to talk to *me*. Eros cursed under his breath. "You have to be fucking kidding me."

I shook my head. This wasn't real. It couldn't have been. How was Trevon... *Was* Trevon an angel? I swallowed hard and glanced around the room. We needed to get him out of here as

183

DESTINY DIESS

soon as possible. He survived The Chains last time... but once these demons found out he was part angel, they would try to corrupt him mentally.

"We have to get him out of here," I said, unlocking the chain around his neck and wrapping my arm around his torso to lift him to his feet. All my anger and rage disappeared in a matter of seconds and was replaced with pure shock.

"We can't," Eros said quietly beside me. "We have nowhere to bring him."

"We can bring him back to Lust."

Eros snatched my arm, leaned closer to me, and whispered, "There are far too many people there, especially during the ceremony. Someone will find him out and try to kill him."

And, as much as I wanted to bring Trevon somewhere that I could protect him, Lust wouldn't do. I thought hard about who could protect him. Dr. U crossed my mind, but she was out on a date and wouldn't be available until morning. Zane was with Maria and would be back to Lust tomorrow morning for the ceremony.

After taking a deep breath, I pushed him toward Eros. "I know someone in Pride who might be able to help."

Eros hesitated for a moment, then took Trevon from me, lifted his body over his shoulder, and hurried down the walkways with him. I slammed the cage shut and locked it, following Eros. Demons rattled their cages at us, but I ignored them—shutting the lights off and leaving them to wallow in their own damn misery.

This was bad. This was really bad.

Neither of us spoke a word to the guards outside the prison. Trevon continued to mumble the familiar hymn and swayed his head back and forth. When we were far away from any prying ears, I dug my claws into Eros's tricep. "How didn't we know this? How could... how could this happen?"

184

DEMONIC DESIRES

"I knew something was fucked up with him," Eros said. I led us down the path toward Dr. Xiexie's offices. I didn't know if he'd be there, but it was worth a damn shot. "I couldn't sense his demon like I usually can with possessed humans, something was blocking the stench. It had to be his angel blocking it out."

Snow plummeted down around us, the wind picking up. I shook my head, still not understanding. "How couldn't *I* know?" I asked, brows furrowed together. "I've known him for years—since we were children. Why couldn't I sense it?"

Eros shrugged his shoulders. "He must be less than an eighth part angel. One of his great-great-grandparents probably had angel blood."

I blew out a deep breath, watching the air turn white in front of my face, and gazed over Eros's shoulder to see a half-passed out Trevon. His eyes were shining white again, a hazy film over them.

The doors were closed, but the light was on in his office. I ripped open the doors, and we walked into the desolate halls, following the light gleaming out from his office.

Without knocking—which was a mistake—I entered the room. A Lust sat on his desk with her legs spread, watching Dr. Xiexie... do whatever it was that he was doing to her. I made eye contact with him and raised a brow, glancing down for only a moment.

Well... I scratched the back of my head and looked away... okay then.

The Lust glanced at me—her eyes immediately widening—hopped off the desk, and bowed her head to me. "Commander."

"Out," I said, not having time for pleasantries. She pulled up her black lacy panties and hurried out the door behind us. I closed it, and Eros put Trevon down onto the table. "Sorry for interrupting, but we have a problem."

Dr. Xiexie brushed it off like nothing happened and zippered

185

DESTINY DIESS

his pants. Eros looked over at me, worry clear in his big, green eyes. "Are you sure this is a good idea?"

"Yes," I said. Out of all the people in Hell that I knew, I trusted Xiexie the most. He had helped me with my Javier problem—to an extent—and had kept my angel a secret. And it helped that he feared me... even if it was just a tiny bit.

"Trevon," I said. Trevon started mumbling the hymn again and opened his eyes to stare directly at the eggshell-colored ceiling.

Dr. Xiexie sucked in a deep breath. "Heavens..."

I brushed my fingers over Trevon's bicep, moving them back and forth to the beat. "This is my ex-boyfriend who has been possessed by three demons now. I can't bring him back to Lust and I don't have anyone on Earth that can monitor him until tomorrow. I'm asking you to watch him until after the ceremony. If you need to... study him. Just don't hurt him."

Dr. Xiexie walked around the table to stare down into Trevon's eyes. When they locked eyes, Trevon's burned with a stronger intensity—so strong that Xiexie looked away. "He's an angel now? Last time I saw him... he had been badly injured by the demons."

"You saw him before?"

"Dr. Xiexie was the doctor that worked on him when I brought him here," Eros said.

I nodded and glanced at Eros, nervousness building inside of me. I didn't want to leave him here, but I didn't have anywhere else to bring him. T

"I'll do it for you," Dr. Xiexie said. "But... I will need something in return. Hiding someone like *him* in Hell will be a gruesome task as he doesn't have a demon scent to mask his angel."

"Anything," I said.

He looked me dead in the eye. "I need protection."

My brows furrowed. "Protection from what?"

186

DEMONIC DESIRES

A sudden silence came over the room, and I almost shivered. "From what's coming," he said as if he knew something that I didn't. I glanced from him to Eros and back. I wasn't the only one who could sense danger close by. He could feel it too.

"Deal."

CHAPTER 33

We walked through the portal in complete silence. I wanted to cry my eyes out because this shit was damn hard, but I couldn't get myself to shed a tear—not when people already thought of me as weak. I stepped through the portal to meet Esha's stoic stare. "What's wrong?" I asked, jaw twitching.

My sadness was slowly transforming me into a wrathful bastard, and I couldn't get myself to care. Not right now.

Esha shook her head, opening the door for me to exit. "Nothing is wrong. I just wanted to make sure you were okay." She gave me a small smile, her tight black uniform pressed against her body from the wind.

"I'm fine," I said, looking over at Chastion as we walked toward the castle. While almost every city light was on, Rebel was amongst the brightest buildings in the city, glowing high in the deep pink night sky. "Watch Chastion tonight. Alert me if anything drastic happens."

After nodding her head, she deviated from the stone walkway and headed toward the town. I pressed my lips together and tried to ignore the stares from some Lusts on their way from other

DEMONIC DESIRES

towns to Chastion. I didn't have the time nor the self-control to listen to another insult and not do anything about it.

Kasey had stirred up more than enough trouble to get people to distrust me, just by walking into my party. Everyone from tonight must've been in the city, talking shit about me now. About how weak I was. About how I couldn't rule. About how I'd never live up to my father's reputation.

I wrapped my arms around myself, feeling another gust of wind from Pride and feeling so... alone. Why the fuck was this happening now? Why couldn't it happen later? Tomorrow night? The next day?

Palace guards opened the doors for me, and I walked into the room, heading straight for the bar where Luci and Jasmine were still talking. I needed something to pick me up, and I knew just the damn thing.

"Dani, you need to relax," Eros said, his hand on the small of my back.

"How am I supposed to calm down?" I tore myself away from him and glared deep into his soft, green eyes. "First Kasey ruins the party. Next I find Trevon in my fucking office trying to take my father's journal. Then I find out he has been possessed again by Samantha!" I inched closer to him and lowered my voice. "And did you forget that he's half fucking angel?!"

My heart raced, and I tried to calm down. I really, really did. But all I could think about was that tomorrow would be a literal shit-show because someone was trying to get dirt on me, someone was going to try to hurt me, steal my crown, and then take my kingdom.

Eros placed his hands on my hips, fingers rubbing small circles on my skin. "Dani," he said, his voice so soft it was almost angelic. "Look at me."

After taking another deep breath, I gazed up at him. A strand of his hair was curled on his forehead, his eyes shifted from a

DESTINY DIESS

deep green to an even deeper black, his plump lips were curled into a smile.

My brows furrowed, and I took a deep breath—suppressing Javier. "How am I supposed to calm down?" I asked again. "Javier hasn't left me alone. From the moment Kasey walked into this room, he wanted me to slaughter everyone in it." I shook my head. "All I wanted was for this one night to go smoothly because I know that tomorrow won't."

He grasped my chin softly, fingers brushing against my jaw. "Just because tonight didn't go as you planned doesn't mean that tomorrow will end badly."

"Better it happen tonight than tomorrow," Lucifer called from the bar. Both he and Jasmine were gazing in my direction, Luci with his signature smile and Jasmine with a sorrowful one. Lucifer took another sip of his drink. "Because *that* would've been a sight to see."

I rolled my eyes and balled my hands into fists against Eros's chest. Luci just didn't know when to shut the hell up, did he? Eros grasped my chin again and made me look up at him. "You are not losing your kingdom tomorrow," he said with such confidence that I actually believed him. He rested his forehead on mine. "Someone might challenge you for your place, but you will not lose it."

His cinnamon drifted through my nose, and I relaxed even further in his hold. "Help me relax," I whispered into his chest. "I just want a peaceful night tonight."

Eros grabbed my hand and guided me toward the bar. "Two Passion Delights." I slid onto the seat next to him and rested my elbow against the counter to gaze at him. Jasmine slid a Passion Delight across the bar. I sipped it quickly, the alcohol going right to my head and making me feel so damn good.

"Your commander is stressed, Jasmine," Lucifer said. "Why don't you help her out?"

As soon as the words left his mouth, I tensed. Jasmine walked

190

around the bar behind me and placed her soft, small hands on my shoulders, digging her thumbs into my back muscle. I glanced at Lucifer, then at Eros's hazy green eyes, then I rolled my shoulders forward and sighed.

"Commander, you're so tense," Jasmine said, breasts brushing against my back. She slipped one of her hands under my dress straps and swiftly pushed it off my shoulder. Eros brushed his foot against the inside of my calf under the bar, and I took a deep breath, inhaling the intoxicating cinnamon, apple, and chocolate-y mixture.

God, they knew exactly what they were doing.

"Relax," she whispered into my ear. I swallowed hard, her arousal so damn strong that I couldn't even think straight. She pushed the other strap off my shoulder, her nose in my hair. "You don't want to be stressed for tomorrow, do you?"

Eros slipped his hand between my legs, rubbing small, tortuous circles against the inside of my thigh. Lucifer chuckled and threw back the rest of his shot.

"How long have you been thinking about this?" Jasmine whispered in my ear, wrapping her hands around my torso and brushing her fingertips against my hardened nipples through my dress. Moment by moment my dress was sliding down my breasts. I sucked in a breath, letting her trial her nails back and forth over them. A wave of pleasure rolled through me, and I moaned when she tugged on them.

My nipples poked right through the silky red dress, and I pressed my thighs together. Eros slid his knee between my legs and scooted to the edge of his seat to rub me through my underwear. "Take it off of her, Jasmine," he said.

Jasmine trailed her fingers over the neckline of my dress and slid them down my breasts to my torso. His sweet scent filled my nostrils and made me clench even harder. Lucifer set his glass on the bar and walked between us. "Now we're talking." He took my nipples between his fingers and pulled me off the seat.

DESTINY DIESS

And, then, he sat in my seat and pulled me onto his lap. His cock was pressed hard against my ass, and he took my breasts in his hand, fondling them lightly. He trailed his lips up the column of my neck, sucking gently on the skin below my ear. "Jasmine was telling me how much she wanted to play with your tight, wet pussy tonight."

My breath caught in the back of my throat, my eyes widening at her. She drew a finger up my thigh, bunching my dress up by my hips. I gazed between her and Eros, my heart pounding in my ears. He stood up and walked beside me, grasping my jaw in one hand and pulling my dress up with the other.

"Would you like that, Dani?" he mumbled against my lips. Jasmine brushed her fingers up the inside of my thighs, getting so close to my pussy yet she didn't touch me. Eros forced me to look up at him, his hazy black eyes driving me wild. "She's not going to touch you until you answer me."

I glanced at her, watching her eyes filled with pure black sin. "Yes," I breathed.

Eros curled his lips into a smirk. "I bet your pussy is aching for her to touch it, isn't it?" He trailed his hand up my other thigh and grasped Jasmine's hand, pulling it to my wet panties. They touched me at the same time, rubbing my clit through the material. "Your panties are ruined for her."

Lucifer tugged on my nipples, pressing his hardness against my ass, and I let out another moan. Eros released Jasmine's hand —letting Jasmine slip her fingers under the material and rub my clit. Pleasure pumped through my entire body, and I curled my toes. God, this couldn't get any better.

Eros wrapped his hand around my throat. "Touch yourself."

I slipped two fingers into my pussy and curled them exactly how I liked it. Lucifer took my other hand and placed it on Eros's cock. I stroked him as quickly as I thrust my fingers into myself, wave after wave of pleasure rolling through me.

192

DEMONIC DESIRES

"Put your fingers into Jasmine's mouth and ask her if you taste good," Lucifer said, tugging on my nipples again.

Jasmine moved her fingers faster around my clit, and I clenched. I pulled my fingers out of me, and Jasmine eagerly accepted them in her mouth to suck off my juices. "Do I taste good?" I asked her. She closed her eyes in pure bliss. When she moaned in response. I brushed a finger across her bottom lip. "Then eat my pussy."

She crouched between my legs and placed her hot mouth on my clit, her tongue flicking out against it. I gripped onto Eros's forearm, digging my claws into him, as I stared down at her. She pressed her mouth closer to me and slid her hands up my trembling legs. Eros ran his fingers down the column of my neck, and I stroked him faster—the pressure in my core rising.

Jasmine brushed her fingers against my entrance, then pushed them inside of me, her mouth still pressed against my clit. Lucifer grinded his cock against my backside harder and groaned against my ear. "Ride her fingers, Dani."

I closed my eyes and moved my hips ever so slowly against her fingers. "Faster," Eros said. I slipped my hand into his pants, taking out his dick, and moved my hips even faster. Jasmine rammed her fingers up into me, tongue flicking against my clit.

"Oh, God," I moaned, the mere friction against my clit driving me wild. Eros placed his lips on my neck, right where he knew melted me each time. A wave of pleasure rolled through me, my pussy tightened around her fingers.

"Make sure she's wet for us," Lucifer said, slapping my breast.

Jasmine moved her fingers faster, and I stopped—trying to squirm away from her, the pressure being too much. Too... damn... much.

"Stay on it," Eros said, hand tightening around my throat. "Cum all over her fingers. I want to taste it." And, as soon as those words left his mouth, I screamed to the high heavens. A leg-trem-

DESTINY DIESS

bling, toe-curling, body tingling orgasm ripped through my body, and I slowly relaxed against Lucifer.

Jasmine licked her lips and pulled out her fingers. Eros grabbed her tiny wrist and sucked her fingers into his mouth. His eyes turned an even hazier black, and he groaned. After he licked off all my juices, he picked me up—bridal style—and walked to the stairs to our bedroom with Lucifer *and* Jasmine close behind him.

Eros tore off my dress and bent me over the side of the bed while Lucifer laid back on the bed, pushed down his pants, and took his cock in his hand. I eagerly wrapped my hand around it and sucked him into my mouth, bobbing my head up and down on him. He reached for Jasmine's hips and pulled her on top of him, pushing her panties out of the way and placing his mouth on her core.

"Spread your legs wider, Dani," Eros said, stepping between my legs and rubbing the head of his cock against my entrance. I spread my legs for him and closed my eyes. He placed sloppy wet kisses down my back, then wrapped his hand into my hair and pushed my head down on Lucifer's cock until it hit the back of my throat. Eros slid into my wet pussy, and I clenched onto him.

Oh, my God, he felt good. Almost too good after everything that had happened tonight.

Lucifer groaned against Jasmine's pussy as Eros bobbed my head up and down on him. Eros started thrusting hard into me from behind until my knees buckled. He wrapped his arm around my waist and held me up, his fingers teasing my clit.

I threw my head back and parted my lips. "Please, more!"

Eros pushed my head back down on Lucifer's cock, forcing him all the way down my throat. My pussy continued to clench around him, becoming tighter and tighter. My nipples brushed against Lucifer's thighs with each thrust, and I moaned on him again, my pussy pulsing.

DEMONIC DESIRES

Eros gripped my hair roughly and pulled me up, pressing his lips against my ear. "Get on the bed."

I crawled onto the bed and positioned Lucifer's cock against my pussy. I slid down on his cock, pleasure rolling through me. Eros spit on his fingers, rubbed them against my ass, and then positioned himself behind me. He slowly pushed himself into me, and the pressure rose in my core. I rested my hands on Jasmine's shoulders and arched my back, letting them thrust up into me.

"Fuck, Dani..." Eros groaned against my ear. My pussy clenched, and I teetered on the edge of another orgasm. Jasmine took my face in her hands and pressed her lips to mine, her tongue slipping into my mouth, her hands playing with my breasts.

Any moment... any damn moment and I would—She flicked my nipples with her fingertips, and I collapsed into her, moaning into her mouth. Wave after wave of pleasure rolled out of me as I felt Eros still inside of me.

Tingles shot up and down my thighs, my mind hazy as I inhaled their scents. Lucifer groaned and pulled out of me, immediately cumming all over his stomach. I rested my head on Jasmine's shoulder and slipped my hand over her core, rubbing softly. "Cum."

Her petite body started shaking uncontrollably, and she threw her head back and screamed, her pussy dripping all over Lucifer's mouth. When she finished, I took a deep breath and rolled off of Lucifer, lying in bed next to Eros and staring up at the ceiling.

God, I might've been half-angel, but *that*... that was something I'd sin for over and over and over again.

CHAPTER 34

𝒫ink sunlight flooded in through our bedroom curtains, and I pulled the blankets over my head, hoping for one more hour of peace. In the distance, I could hear the rumble of demons in Chastion, preparing for today. I blew out a deep breath, my stomach in tight knots.

The bed dipped beside me, and I turned onto my side and wrapped my arm around Eros's unusually thin waist. "Please don't leave yet, Eros," I grumbled into his stomach. "I'm not ready for today."

He pulled the blankets down and brushed his fingers against my cheek, his touch softer and so much gentler than usual. "Dani," a woman said. I blinked my eyes open, adjusting to the light, and stared up at Jasmine. A silky purple robe clung to her body, and her hair was pulled into a ponytail. She smiled at me. "Good morning."

"Jasmine," I whispered, her name rolling off my lips so easily. Memories of last night flooded through my mind, and I relaxed into the plush sheets and curled my fingers around her waist. "Come back to bed."

"Today's the day," she said. "You will officially become queen."

I frowned and groaned internally. "Don't remind me."

She playfully slapped my shoulder. "Stop it. You'll be amazing." Tingles erupted over my skin. She nodded to a breakfast tray topped with Lust's finest Fervor Crisps, bacon, and strudel sitting on my nightstand. "I made you breakfast. There should be enough for you and them." She glanced at Eros and Lucifer behind me.

Eros laid on his side, his fingers curled around my waist. Lucifer laid beside him on his back, head tilted toward Eros's hair, breathing in his scent deeply. I eyed their proximity; something about it was so natural that I knew it had to have happened before.

Jasmine stood, but I grasped her wrist and sat up. "Thank you," I whispered, resting my head against the headboard and smiling. "It really means a lot to me." To have someone in Hell, someone in *Lust* who cared about me... it felt nice.

Her gaze flickered to my lips, and I brushed my fingers against hers, the same sinful desire from last night filling my entire body again.

Something about the way she looked at me... the same way that Eros looked at me before we started dating. It made me all giddy inside. And while I knew what I wanted for once in my life —her for more than just one night—I had promised Eros that we wouldn't date anyone else until our kingdom was under control. And our kingdom was far from *under control* right now.

My gaze flickered to the closed curtains, and I dropped my hand. "Go," I said hesitantly. I didn't want her to leave, but if she didn't leave now, I wouldn't be able to ask her to leave later.

When she left, I grabbed a crisp from the breakfast tray and bit into it, hoping it'd ease my anxiety. Something would happen today, something that even *I* wouldn't be able to stop.

Belial knew it. Dad knew it. Dr. Xiexie knew it. I knew it.

Whether it would be the outcry of the people from not believing in me or the Unholy Trinity who'd make their appearance, I had to stay strong. I brushed my fingers against my ring and a burst of warmth spread through my body. My mind filled with memories I hadn't ever experienced before.

Memories of Mom and Dad.

Meeting each other for the first time in Crimson's Nouveau. Spending one sinful night under Lust's rosy night skies. The look of pure joy on Mom's face when Dad slid her ring onto her finger. Dad's overwhelming emotions when Mom told him she was pregnant with me.

I didn't know what it was, but I wanted to believe that they were here with me today, through it all. A tear slid down my cheek, and I quickly pushed it away. Eros shifted next to me and reached for a Fervor Crisp on my plate. He smiled up at me with tired eyes. "Good morning, *my little succubus.*"

Eros sat up next to me, his shoulder brushing against mine, and pressed his lips to my forehead. "You shouldn't be crying," he said to me. "This should be the best day of your life."

I rested my head on his shoulder and brushed my fingers over the ring again, hoping for another memory but not experiencing one. It was like that memory didn't exist anymore, but, for the shortest moment that it did, it made me feel things I hadn't felt since Mom died.

"It is," I said. Because Mom and Dad were watching over me—wherever they were.

After a few moments of silence, Lucifer groaned next to Eros. "Why must it be so warm in Lust all the time? It feels like Heaven."

I picked a green apple off the breakfast tray and tossed it to Lucifer. "Jasmine brought you an apple." The apple landed on Luci's covered stomach. He tore the blankets off of him, stood up completely naked, and tossed the apple into the air. Instead of pulling on some pants, he walked right over to the balcony, pushed the doors open, and stepped out into the sun.

DEMONIC DESIRES

Eros intertwined my fingers with his and brushed his thumb across my ring. "One day, I'll get you one of our own."

My eyes widened, my heart suddenly pumping with excitement. Eros wanted... to get me a wedding ring? Something to symbolize us? A smile stretched across my lips, my emotions all over the damn place this morning.

"Dani has a crowd today," Lucifer said, leaning over the balcony and ruining the goddamn moment. "Didn't think there'd be this many people here."

After pressing my lips to Eros's, I wrapped a robe over my body and walked out onto the balcony to gaze over the edge. Hundreds and hundreds of demons were pouring out of Chastion, filling the walkways, and heading straight to the palace to get a spot to view the Courting Pit.

"God..." I whispered.

"She can't help you down here," Lucifer said, chuckling. He noticed a couple people down below and cursed under his breath. "I'll see you at the ceremony. I have to take care of some things."

When Luci left, Eros grabbed another Fervor Crisp, broke it into two pieces, and handed me one. He wrapped his arms around me from behind and stared down at the demons below. "They're all here for you," he said in my ear. "Don't be nervous."

"I'm terrified. Absolutely terrified."

"Remember what I told you at the skating rink," Eros said, feeding me his crisp. "You're the strongest of them all. You have nothing to worry about. Believe in yourself." He placed his lips below my ear. "Because *you* will be queen."

I smoothed out my red silk dress in the mirror and tried my hardest to smile at my reflection. But with every passing moment, my stomach tightened. How many people would challenge me for my throne today? How many people would I have to prove wrong? What would I really have to do to show everyone that I was the only queen that could sit on my father's throne?

Eros curled his fingers into my side, his cinnamon scent wrapping around me like a comfort blanket. Standing in a fitted suit with horns glistening under the sun and eyes impeccably dark, he grinned at my reflection. "It's time."

After turning around to face him for the last time before I became queen, I tried steadying my quivering lips. "Do you promise to stay by me the entire time and for all the years to come?"

He grasped my hands and pressed his lips to my knuckles, kissing me the same way he did the first time I met him in that old apartment. "I promise." And, then, he guided me to the ground floor. More guards than usual stood around the inside of the palace. Even through these thick walls, I could hear the crowd of people chatting outside.

When we reached the palace doors, Esha looked at me. "Are we ready to begin?"

All I wanted to do was run back upstairs, lock myself in our bedroom, and wish this day away. But instead, I smiled and nodded my head. Sure, I was ready…

The guards opened the double doors, and sunlight flooded into the room. I stood just out of sight, still in the shadows of the palace. God, give me strength. I took a deep breath and stepped into the light, feeling the warmth immediately on my bare skin.

Eros took my hand and led me down the palace steps. Demons from all kingdoms were standing on the steps, being held back by Lust guards. They were lined up on the walkways, trying so hard to glimpse at me. My heart pounded in my chest, and I squeezed Eros's hand tighter, carefully trying not to trip over my own feet, tumble down the stairs, and make a fool out of myself.

There was a grand walkway from the stairs, around the castle,

DEMONIC DESIRES

and toward the Courting Pit—which was right outside the throne room. Demons stared at me, and I kept eye contact with them, hoping I wasn't giving off any fear. And, finally, after walking for what seemed like forever, we reached a colosseum-looking structure.

Every blood-sucking, flesh-eating monstrosity in Hell filled the stadium made from marble and stone, standing at least ten stories in the air. The walls to the throne room had been knocked down, and there was a red velvet carpet leading from the center of the colosseum to the throne itself. Lusts' ruby red crown sat on the throne, a hazy black mist drifting around its tines.

I swallowed hard and hesitated right by the entrance as the crowd suddenly quieted down. In the center, there were six large golden chairs—supplied by Greed—where the other six commanders sat, their heirs sitting in the first row of seating.

When Lucifer saw us, he stood and smirked. "May I present you Dani Asmodeus."

Well, this was it. I brushed my fingers against my parents' ring. I would not let them down. I hooked my arm around Eros's and walked toward the center of the stadium. Thousands upon thousands of eyes were fixed on *me,* and an unsettling feeling sat heavily in the air.

Kasey and the nasty rumors she had started flashed into my mind. I glanced around, trying to find her minions, when my eyes landed on Maeve. She smiled at me from the first row, where my court was seated, her eyes an excited green. They were calming.

Lucifer started the ceremony off with a few traditional speeches about the original seven fallen angels turned commanders. I shifted from foot to foot, glancing at my throne and back into the crowd, hoping to spot someone who'd challenge me so I could prepare. But after an hour, I couldn't find anyone or anything out of place.

201

DESTINY DIESS

"And, now..." Lucifer started. "Does anyone wish to challenge Dani, *the rightful heir to the throne,* for her kingdom?"

Everyone quieted down—not a single word being spoken in this entire crowd. My heart pounded against my ribcage, and I took deep breaths through my nose. My gaze shifted from commander to commander, to section after section, waiting for someone to ruin this day for me. But nobody spoke a single word.

Not Biast.

Not Sathanus.

Not the Envy Queen.

Not anyone... until her.

Maeve stood up from my court. "I do."

CHAPTER 35

My eyes widened, betrayal stabbing me right in the damn heart. What the fucking hell was she doing?

Maeve stood up from her seat and stared at Lucifer. "I challenge Dani for the throne."

God, I should've seen this coming and I should've trusted Kasey. But I was blinded with betrayal and hurt. And now, I'd pay for it.

Eros tensed behind me, looking more confused than I was. The silent crowd suddenly burst out into a cheer. Demons were hooting and hollering, screaming at the top of their lungs, waiting for some action.

If I could just stay calm enough until she made her first move, I could defeat her easily. We wouldn't have any more trouble. Javier... Javier wouldn't lose control.

"Quiet," I shouted, rage building high inside of me. Every demon in the entire stadium became deathly quiet again, sensing my wrath. Even Sathanus sat back in his seat, looking at me as if he recognized me as Javier himself.

Eros grabbed my wrist before I could step forward and accept the challenge. "Dani, be careful."

I snatched my arm away from him, my jaw twitching. If she wanted to challenge me, then I would accept it. I had to. I would not accept defeat or give up my father's dreams for me. This kingdom was mine.

"Melinda," Maeve called, turning toward the crowd. All the way at the top of the stadium, someone stood. Maeve curled her lip into an evil snarl at me and said, "Bring her."

Melinda walked down the stairs toward us, holding a chain tightly in her hand and dragging a woman behind her. The woman—so weak—couldn't stand on her own. Her knees were bloody, her body smacking over and over against the concrete stairs, leaving a trail of sanguine blood.

When she reached the ground, my heart dropped. I shook my head and stepped back, bumping into Eros. No... No, this couldn't be happening. That wasn't just any woman... it was Dr. U, the one woman who had sacrificed her life to raise me.

Heavy silver chains were wrapped around her wrists and her neck. Both of her eyes were swollen shut. Purple bruises and dirt, open gashes and blood covered almost every inch of her body. I parted my lips to shriek, but nothing would come out.

All I could feel was an intense pain and a growing rage.

Melissa—who had been Dr. U's pretty pink-haired date—threw Dr. U to the ground like she was nothing. Something inside of me snapped when she fell face first onto the concrete in front of all the other commanders. I growled and lurched forward, ready to kill them both, but Eros grasped my hand and pulled me back. "Dani," he whispered into my ear. "Don't act off your emotions. They want you to get angry."

Dr. U's cute dress was soaked with red blood and had been ripped in seven different places. This was my fault. All my fault. If she had never found me, she wouldn't be here right now. She would be at work, living her life to the fullest. Not in Hell, facing death head on.

DEMONIC DESIRES

"Thanks to Melissa," Maeve said, eyes twinkling green with envy. "We've found out who Dani Asmodeus really is."

My stomach tightened, but this time I didn't feel that constant tug of anxiety. This was it... the beginning of the end. Everything was about to go downhill from here, I could just feel it. I clenched my fists by my side, eyes flickering from Maeve to Dr. U.

Dr. U gazed up at me. "I'm sorry, Dani." Her voice sounded so fragile. "She went through all my pap—"

"Quiet!" Melissa said. "Or I'll hang you out your office window again."

My jaw twitched, a growl ripping its way out of my throat. My vision blurred, and I saw red. Red blood from Dr. U. Red eyes from Mom's killer. Red. Red. Red. Red. Red. I ripped myself out of Eros's grip. Rage swelled inside of me, and I licked my fangs.

"She's trying to make you look weak," Eros said. "Don't give into her."

But she was about to tell my damn secret to everyone in Hell and she had hurt Dr. U, I wouldn't be a coward this time. I stared right at her and grazed my finger against my family ring, feeling so damn torn. Mom was telling me to calm down, Dad was telling me to fight, and Javier was telling me to surrender control.

I knew that if I lost control, I wouldn't be able to stop this time. And that freaked me out almost as much as everyone knowing that I was part angel. But it wasn't only that...

Dr. U was here. If I lost control... I might hurt her. I might kill her. And if I didn't, someone else might. I couldn't risk it, not when we were surrounded by thousands of demons, not when Maeve was about to spill my darkest secret, not when Dr. U was the only family I had left.

"Take Maeve to The Chains," I said through clenched teeth,

"This is the Courting Pit," Lucifer said, leaning my way. "This is where people challenge you. Nobody can nor will be brought to The Chains."

Maeve cleared her throat. "Look at her empty threats," she

DESTINY DIESS

said. "She can't bring me to The Chains, she can't hurt me, she can't even kill me because the thought plagues her mind."

Dr. U weakly pushed herself to her hands and knees. "Stop," she said, voice frail and hoarse.

"Your soon-to-be commander is weak because she is not only Asmodeus's child..." Maeve smirked at me and spoke to the crowd. "But her mother is Fatima, the angel who stole Asmodeus's heart and made him weak."

A deafening silence erupted through the crowd, but the thoughts in my head were loud. *"Kill her... kill her now."* They were driving me wild, savage, feral. *"Take her soul."*

My jaw twitched again. Every moment, it was getting harder and harder to control myself. I needed to figure out a way to protect Dr. U. Somehow, someway. She laid there so helplessly beneath vile creatures she shouldn't have ever had to meet.

"An angel cannot rule our kingdom," someone said from the crowd, breaking through the silence.

I had tried to prepare for this uproar... But the words still cut me like a Wrath's claws. People didn't believe a half-angel had what it took to lead Hell. My gaze shifted from Dr. U to the commanders to the entire crowd, locking onto Biast. With his tail curled in the air and his devilish red eyes focused on me, he smirked.

This was a big fucking game to him. He wanted me to destroy myself... and it happened. He didn't even need to lift a damn finger for me to screw everything up before it even began... that was, if I wasn't careful.

My gaze drifted back to Dr. U, and I knew exactly what I had to do.

"Protect everyone I care about," I said to Eros.

"I'm not leaving your side."

"You can't protect me from this. This is my fight."

Eros clenched his jaw and looked away, his fingers brushing against mine. "Okay."

206

I pushed my shoulders back and stepped forward. "Let me speak," I growled. The crowd continued to erupt into fits of howling. Javier clawed at my insides, wanting all demons to face our wrath and to know what I really was capable of.

When nobody quieted down, I growled louder. The people who hadn't lost faith in me turned toward me and bowed their heads in respect. But the ones who didn't continued to spew hate in my direction.

"Quiet!" I shouted, my voice booming through the stadium. More and more demons eventually quieted down, and I stared between everyone who had betrayed me, then finally stared at my *best friend* Maeve. "How could you all think my father was weak?" I asked, nostrils flaring. "He was one of the first seven angels to fall from the Heavens. He ruled Hell for thousands and thousands of years before an Envy stole his kingdom from him. And that fucking Envy barely ruled for two decades before her own son killed her."

More memories of my father—of falling from the Heavens, of the pain that ran through every fiber of his being as he slammed onto the grounds of Lust, of the moment he was crowned as king —ran through my mind. Something about standing here, in this very spot, being bashed by demons who didn't even know me and my power... it made me feel things that only a commander like my father would have felt before.

A lustful desire to rule. An undeniable urge to make the people obey. Power.

His ring clutched down harder on my finger—refusing to be moved. I took another step forward. "My father was not weak, and neither am I."

"You're an angel," someone else shouted from the crowd, which earned him an uproar of nods and comments aimed at me from only some demons this time.

I tried hard to control my wrath, but with every moment that passed, I could feel it building inside of me, almost as strong as

DESTINY DIESS

my lust. "Yes, I am half-angel and I am half-demon. I'm good. I'm bad." *I'm hungry.* "But I will defend my kingdom and my birthright, my father and my mother, from anyone who wants to step in my way. I will be the strongest queen to ever lead our kingdom."

CHAPTER 36

A look of fear crossed Maeve's face when most of the crowd didn't oppose me this time. They believed in me... at least, most of them did. And the ones who didn't were hesitant to speak. She stepped forward, pointing a sharp claw at me. "How can we trust an angel to rule Hell?"

I stared at her, finally calming myself down enough to think straight. Maeve had raised an army of my people and fixed them against me. She betrayed me, just like Kasey said she would. And I was a damn fool to believe that an Envy could ever want to be my loyal friend without wanting something more.

Eros stayed beside me, unmoving, yet he kept his eye on Dr. U who sat on her hands and knees in a puddle of her own blood. I clenched my hands into fists and glanced down at her in sorrow. Courting Pit, my ass... this turned out to be a riot to overthrow me.

"Get her off the throne," one of Maeve's louder accomplices said to stir up trouble.

"She doesn't deserve it."

"Mother sent her here to weaken Hell."

My heart pounded at the sea of people who were angrily

DESTINY DIESS

turning on me. Out of the thousands of people here, there were only about a hundred demons who still didn't think I was fit to rule... but it was a hundred *Lust* demons. A hundred of my own kind.

Lucifer stepped closer to me.

"They think you're weak, Dani," Lucifer whispered into my ear. "They want to take the throne from you. Don't think you're fit to rule the kingdom. They want to watch you burn in the pits of Wrath."

My jaw twitched, watching Maeve—my friend—continue to rile up her followers. Javier's wrath became my own. Lust and wrath filled me, snapping me into the queen I truly was, and overtaking me with such viciousness that even the Javier in me paused.

"If you don't prove yourself now, this will happen in the coming years," Lucifer said.

And when the devil talked in my ear, I listened because he told the truth. Maeve and her minions needed to be eliminated. Eliminated today. By me.

"Show them who you are," Lucifer said. *"Make them fear you."*

Maeve looked me right in the eye with a grand smirk on her face, thinking she'd get out of this alive. "You will burn in Tartarus, *Commander...*" She walked toward Dr. U. "But before you do, you will watch your closest family die right before your eyes. And even your heavenly Mother won't be able to save her."

She lifted her arm into the air, pointing her claws right toward Dr. U's neck, and thrust them toward her. My body seemed to move without direction, grand wings spurting from my back. I collapsed over Dr. U's body and shielded her from Maeve's claws.

Her talons dug deep into my back, ripping my flesh, and I took the pain. I held Dr. U to my chest. "Nothing will happen to you," I whispered. "Eros will protect you." And, then, I thrust my

210

DEMONIC DESIRES

wings back—sending Maeve flying across the stadium—and shoved Dr. U into Eros's arms.

A collective gasp echoed through the air. Maeve hit the concrete walls, the pure force of the impact making some stone crumble over her when she landed on the ground. She rolled onto her hands and knees and shrieked. "She'll protect anyone from our scorn!" she yelled. "Kill her!"

Her followers ran down the stairs, hopped over the first row's warriors, and sprinted at me, howling through razor-sharp teeth and running with talons that could *try* to rip me to shreds. Maeve stumbled to her feet and ran toward the throne room, her green eyes fixed on my crown.

"*Take their souls,*" Javier said inside of me. "*Suck them out. Feel their power through your veins. Make them suffer.*"

And, for once in my entire life, I wasn't terrified of his voice... because it wasn't Javier's voice. It was mine. I was the monster and I revelled in it.

I sprinted toward Maeve, and my wings lifted me off the ground. She staggered into the throne room and up the velvet carpet. A power built within me, a hunger crawling up the back of my throat, wanting to be filled with her soul. Just as she reached for my crown, I flew into the room and grasped her by the throat to pull her into the air with me.

She let out a shrill cry, and I couldn't hold back my lust anymore. I pressed my lips to hers, the carnal need to feel her gasping for air overwhelmingly strong. My hand tightened around her pretty little throat. And I sucked.

All I could hear were her whimpers and the sound of demons approaching me from behind. All I could feel were her claws digging into my chest to push me away. All I could taste was lavender.

The pressure rose inside of me, the intoxicating pleasure pumping through my body. Her eyes widened, and she made one last attempt to escape my grasp. And, then, I heard the crack.

211

Could feel her fragile neck snap in my palm. I sucked her soul right from her body and inhaled it—wanting to savor the moment. Her envy, her jealousy, her life flowed through my veins, and I groaned softly.

It almost felt better than when Eros stroked my horns.

When her arms fell limply at her sides, I dropped her from my grasp and watched her fall onto the floor of the throne room. Her head bounced off the stone floors, blood seeping out of her wound. I floated to the ground and smirked at her, a hazy film blurring my vision.

My tongue slid across my fangs. I needed more.

Maeve's minions leapt at me from behind, sinking their fangs into my neck, digging their claws into my flesh, wrapping their tails around my legs to try to hold me in place. And, so, I grasped the closest traitor, curled my hand around his neck, and tasted just how sweet his life was on my lips.

I inhaled his soul, feeling that strength of life, that will to live, that fear of death. A surge of power swelled inside of me, and I let his body fall to the ground. *"More."* I reached behind me and yanked one over my shoulder, pressing my lips to hers.

One demon here, two there, five out in the court. God, I needed more.

Bodies fell into piles around me. Commanders stared at me with wide eyes. Demons in the stadium hurried to leave in a panic. My eyes locked onto Sathanus and his tasty-looking lips, but I knew I wouldn't be able to get close enough now. I needed to feed. I had been starved.

Someone grabbed my hand from behind and turned me around. I licked my fangs, ready to taste the man's lips, but then I saw Eros. Eyes a wide green, a touch so gentle, lips so damn tempting. My claws dug into his forearms, and I pulled him closer. I growled in hunger for him, for his soul, for it to bind with mine.

He brushed his fingers against my cheek, and for a moment, I

DEMONIC DESIRES

leaned into his touch and tilted my head into his hand. That's when I saw *him*. Biast. Standing a few feet away. Dark, dangerous eyes on me. A sinful, monstrous look on his face. I grabbed Eros's chin, smiled sweetly at him, and placed a kiss on his lips. "I love you." And then I pushed him out of the way and hurried toward Biast, the need building inside of me more than anything ever had.

When I grabbed Biast by the throat, he wrapped his tail around my ankle—holding me close. There wasn't a single ounce of fear in his eyes, but an unusual sort of... pride. I didn't waste time overthinking it. Instead, I pressed my lips to his—wanting to just kill him right then and there.

Biast didn't struggle. He didn't claw or scream or yell. He rested his hands almost softly on my hips and kissed me back, his tongue tangling with mine as if he was enjoying this. And... I wasn't going to lie... I enjoyed it too. More than I should have.

After a few moments, I pulled away from him, absolutely breathless. Something was wrong. Why couldn't I take his soul? He licked his lips and unwrapped his tail. "Can't kill me either, Commander, can you?"

Without wasting another breath on him, I pushed him out of the way and decided to feed on someone else. There were plenty of traitors, plenty of men and women who wanted to witness my fall.

Unable to control myself, I grabbed whoever I could. I needed more. More life. More lust. More of everything. The intoxicating scents of my people—whether they were trying to flee from me or running toward me to try to ruin me—smelt too good. And when I inhaled the familiar scent of chocolate, I grabbed a woman by her waist and pressed my lips to hers.

She struggled in my hold, pressing her hands into my chest. Someone pulled me off her and stepped between us. "Dani..." Though my vision was blurry, I could sense Eros. "Dani, you don't want to hurt Jasmine."

DESTINY DIESS

My heart stopped at the sound of her name, my vision returning for only a second to see Jasmine's wide eyes at me. With red fingerprints on her neck, she was gasping for air in Eros's arms. I muttered an apology, but couldn't stop myself from licking my lips again at the mere sight of her. "Protect her, Eros. Protect her from me because I can't control this."

And I didn't want to.

When I turned back around, the crowd had started to diminish. One person at a time.

I grabbed onto the nearest man—Axel, Maeve's lover—and pressed my lips to his. My wings lifted me into the air, my lust becoming stronger by the moment. It took only a second to kill him, to snap his neck, and to inhale his life essence.

He slipped from my hands, and a sense of satiety washed over me. I gazed down at the sea of perished demons below me, who had been vying for my crown. A horrific chuckle escaped my lips, and I floated back to the ground.

Lucifer stood around the litter of bodies, lips curled into a smirk. Biast sat on one of the Throne Room couches with Maeve in his arms, fangs sunk deep into her flesh, feasting on her blood. The souls of my victims bound to mine, becoming one with me.

I walked to my throne, picked up my crown, and sat. Half-angel, half-demon, all me. The good, the bad, the ugly. Through all the doubts, all the traitors, everything, I crowned my damn self because I was...

Dani Asmodeus.

Queen of Lust.

Commander in Hell.

The most powerful being to step foot into the depths of the Underworld.

And nobody would stop me.

To be continued...

ABOUT THE AUTHOR

Destiny Diess is a paranormal romance author who lives in Pittsburgh, PA. With over 28 million reads online as of June 2020, Destiny enjoys writing books about werewolves, demons, and gods. She's currently writing the Becoming Lust Trilogy.

Printed in the USA
CPSIA information can be obtained
at www.ICGtesting.com
LVHW051031221123
764422LV00006B/1083

9 781734 622348